SERIOUSLY SEXY 3

A collection of twenty erotic stories

Edited by Miranda Forbes

Published by Accent Press Ltd – 2008
ISBN 9781906125905

Copyright © Accent Press Ltd 2008

Printed and bound in the UK

Cover Design by
Red Dot Design

Contents

Twelve new titles for 2008

Bad Girl

Seriously Sexy One

Naughty Spanking One

Tease Me

Down & Dirty One

Seriously Sexy Two

Juicy Erotica

Satisfy Me

Naughty Spanking Two

Seriously Sexy Three

Down & Dirty Two

Seduce Me

For more information please visit
www.xcitebooks.com

Picking The Man
by Penelope Friday

As soon as I enter the pub, I look around and choose my mark, this evening's catch. Tonight … yes, *there*, the guy in the red jumper, short brown hair. He catches my eye and immediately looks away. They all do that at first. Later, well, we'll see if this one changes his response. I order a vodka and orange, and then make my way to the table next to his. Our eyes meet again and he blushes. Mm, shyer than some. More hang-ups than usual? More insecurities? He might be quite a challenge.

I like a challenge.

He's keeping his eyes fixed on the table now, pretending to read the paper, scared to look up. I edge a little closer, and speak.

"Anything interesting in there?"

I hide a smile as he literally jerks with the shock of being addressed by me. He risks a quick glance in my direction, runs a hand through his hair.

"Oh, you know. The usual."

Oh, I picked well this time. He has a beautiful baritone voice with the slightest trace of a Northern accent.

"I don't know." I smile at him. "So tell me." I mirror his movement and brush my right hand through my own hair. As he wavers, I move a little closer. "You know you want to," I murmur.

He is giving me The Look. Some men pick up on me right away, and know exactly where I'm headed. More, though, hesitate. The hesitators all wear exactly the same expression on their faces and I can interpret it precisely.

It sounds like she's flirting with me. Is she? She can't be, but it does sound that way. No, I must be imagining it. She wouldn't flirt. She's in a wheelchair.

The chair, you understand, stops me (in most guys' original assessment) from being a normal functional woman. They learn. They soon learn. I like to think I'm doing my bit for stereotype busting but in actuality, I'm just getting a lot of sex. Which suits me, thanks!

Anyway, back to Mr Red Jumper. I have leaned forward, and my elbows are on his table, my head leaning on my fists as I give him the once-over from a closer perspective. I make no attempt to hide my assessment. Why should I, when he measures up so well? Why should I, when I will be in bed with him later tonight? That assessment will be much fuller, but for the moment I work gently around his prejudices and give him time to get used to the idea.

"Um," he stammers, "fuel prices; the government being criticised for this new housing scheme." He shrugs a little apologetically. "Nothing very interesting."

"Oh, what a shame. But you were studying it so intently that I imagined there must be something fascinating there."

"Afraid not."

"But that's good," I assure him.

"It is?" He looks a little alarmed and I move in for the first small pounce.

"Yes." I smile again, my head tilted to the side. "You see, it means we can dispense with this" – I sweep the paper to the far side of the table – "and get down to business."

He smiles back, uncertainly. I force him to hold my gaze for five – ten – twenty seconds. I don't know what he reads in my face, but the smile becomes more genuine.

"Are you always this forceful?" he asked.

2

"Usually." I sip my drink thoughtfully, and add, "And you're right, you know."

"About what?"

"I *am* flirting with you. Do you mind?"

"Uh …" The shyness I noticed earlier has returned. "I'm not sure anyone's actually come right out with it like that before."

"They probably don't need to. If it weren't for this," I say, patting the wheelchair, "you'd have been sure already."

"I … oh God, you're probably right," he confesses in embarrassment. "Is that dreadful?"

"Fairly common. That's why I tend to be a tad forceful." I wink. "But don't worry."

He thinks I am talking about his stereotyping of me and begins to stammer out an apology. This is good. It gives me a chance to touch him.

"Shh!" I put my finger across his lips. "I didn't mean that. I just meant that circumstances have given me the opportunity to be very much more … creative … than most women. I see it as an advantage, not a disadvantage."

He laughs. He is still a little reserved, but he seems to have relaxed slightly in my company.

"You do like to come straight out with things. I'm Dan, by the way."

"Ellie. It's always useful to know names before having sex with someone, don't you think?"

"Ellie, whatever your name is, you're outrageous. We haven't even kissed!" But the glint in his eye shows that he is considering me now; that he is beginning to see me as a genuine prospect.

"We will," I say.

"I might have a girlfriend."

I shake my head.

"You don't."

"I might."

I laugh now.

3

"You'll have to tell her she's been overtaken by events, then. Sorry and all that, but you've had an offer that you can't turn down."

"And have I?"

"Oh yes," I tell him.

"Good."

And now it is his turn to make a move as he leans across the table and kisses me lightly on the mouth. My lips tingle at the touch, and I know that once more my instinct has not led me astray. Tonight is going to be good.

"You could do that again," I suggest.

"I could," he agrees. He slides round the table so that we are inches apart. "But I could go a little further and do this…"

The kiss this time has nothing of the lightness of the last one. He is demanding, exploring my mouth with his tongue, one hand behind my head to keep me just where he wants me. And believe me, I'm not complaining. His jumper is soft and woolly, but I can feel the strength of the muscles underneath. Dan keeps himself fit, it seems. I slide one hand lower to his waist, hitching the jumper and shirt beneath out of the way to press my fingers against his skin. I trail my nails the length of his back and down again. Finally he pulls away. Now he can meet my eyes with no embarrassment. But he chooses to lean in and whisper in my ear.

"Isn't that sort of behaviour illegal in a public place?"

"Is it?" I ask innocently, removing my hand from his back only to slide it up his thigh. He clamps his own, larger, hand over mine.

"Stop that!"

"Do you really want me to?"

"No," he confesses, "but you can't do it here." He looks meaningfully at our drinks. "It'd be a shame to waste them," he says casually, "but it depends what the alternatives are."

"Drink up, Danny boy," I reply, downing my vodka in

one swift motion. "You're taking me home."

He raises an eyebrow but obediently puts his pint to his lips and takes a gulp. Then he pushes the nearly empty glass to the centre of the table and stands up.

"I can live without the rest," he says, "but you have a promise to keep."

"Me?" I wheel myself to the door, and when we are outside, I say "What promise?"

"Why, to demonstrate your creativity, sweetheart."

I grin. That line is always a winner. My next is intentionally predictable.

"My place or yours?"

He leans down to snog me again, and his hand skims my breast making my nipple stand to attention.

"Whichever's nearer, Ellie," he murmurs.

"Follow me."

My house is less than five minutes from the pub, making it one of my favourite pick-up points. I've never seen Dan there before, though I noticed one or two familiar faces (and more than faces) when I entered tonight. We get home quickly. Dan has been touching me all the way; a hand on my shoulder, fingers combing through my hair. I'm enjoying his eagerness. I unlock the door, go in and spin myself around to face him.

"Welcome to my place."

He is inside, the door slamming shut behind him. He looks around, slightly disconcerted by the décor. I went for bright in the sitting room, and the one scarlet wall contrasts with the cream of the other three to make a real statement. He is silent for a second then turns back to me.

"Red for passion," he says huskily. "Very suitable, Ellie."

I put my right hand up to my blouse and unfasten the top two buttons, no more. I have done the brash 'come hither'; now I prefer a more measured – more slowly seductive – effect. His eyes follow the curve of my breasts, the lacy white bra I am wearing. He wants more. Always leave them wanting more. I hold my hand out to him in mute invitation, and a second later he is by my side, his finger tracing the line of material exposed by my unbuttoning. His other hand rests on my leg and he hesitates.

"I'm not hurting you?"

"You can't," I say truthfully, "but if you do, I promise to yell 'ouch'." The wheelchair effect again. I pull him down for a kiss and then say "Trust me."

"I rather think I do," he says, a smile playing on his lips. Then, "Show me."

It is an invitation I am happy to accept. I can see that he is unsure whether to stand or kneel, and much as I enjoy having men kneel at my feet, anxiety is less erotic.

"Come to bed."

I adore my bed. Once in their lives, everyone should do something outrageously extravagant. For me, it was when I bought my bed. My stunning, perfect, four-poster bed. I watch the effect it has on Dan. Some men blanch, but not he.

"Red for passion, bed for luxury," he says with appreciation. "I like your style."

I tumble onto the centre, teasing fingers playing with the next button of my blouse – unfastening, fastening; unfastening, fastening.

"Join me?" I suggest.

"I intend to."

He removes his jumper and shirt, leaving himself naked to the waist. I whistle appreciatively.

"Not bad," I comment.

"Good enough for the bed?" he asks, and I am turned on by his perception. Not all guys realise the symbolism of my four-poster. I inspect his pecs and nod.

"You'll do."

He has kicked off his shoes, and he kneels at the far end of the bed to remove mine with delicate suggestiveness. I wear no stockings or tights, and he takes the opportunity to play with my feet, licking each toe in turns. I hum with pleasure at the sensation that trickles up my legs and throbs between them.

"You'll more than do," I correct myself.

My skirt is fanned out across the bed, and he makes a tent of it, crawling underneath and licking up the inside of my leg with his tongue until he reaches my sex, until he flicks his tongue against my clit and makes me moan and squirm. When he reappears from under my skirt, I pull him up to me and kiss him, tasting myself on his lips.

"I thought I was the one who'd promised to be creative," I say.

"Complaining?"

"Oh, believe me, not complaining."

He is already hard – very hard indeed, I discover, pulling his body on top of mine and revelling in the feeling. I writhe in my position underneath him and feel him twitch in response. My hands slide round to unlatch his belt; I flick open the top button of his jeans and press my fingers just a tiny way inside. Enough to tantalise, especially when I wriggle my fingers so that the tips just brush against his cock. He pushes his torso up, one hand either side of my head, and looks into my eyes.

"I still like your style," he says, his voice that little bit deeper than before.

Slowly, I lick a path up his jaw line to his ear, and nibble on the lobe.

"I'm rather interested in yours, too," I whisper, and undulate my body against his once more. Then, when he is not expecting it, I roll over so that our positions are reversed: this time I am on top. I tease him with kisses and light bites, squirming further down his body in order to play with his neck. I bite the place where his neck and shoulder meet, and I do not think that the noise he makes when I do so is a complaint. I move further down, and unzip his jeans.

He (like me) is wearing no pants. Interesting: is he as innocent as I first imagined? I rather hope not. I pull the jeans down and over his feet and then look up at him from between his legs.

I know what he is thinking.

I know what he is thinking, but it's not going to happen, not yet. He expects it, anticipates it. I will wait until he is off-guard, until he thinks that this is not something he will get from this encounter. I will taunt and tempt him, but I will not give him what he's looking for. I lower my mouth and press one kiss to his cock, enjoying the way it moves in response. Then I am moving higher again, my tongue exploring his belly button, running over his chest, suckling at his nipple.

I pause, and take the opportunity to divest myself of my skirt, and to undo one further button on my top. His hands are reaching hopefully for the other buttons, but I push myself out of their reach.

"Not yet. Not quite."

"Tease," he mumbles.

I grab one of his hands and suck the first digit into my mouth, swirling it within my mouth as if it were the best ice cream that I desired to savour. The gesture is not lost on him.

"Tease," he says again.

"The night is long," I promise.

And oh, yes, it is. Through that long, hot summer night, the bed rustles and creaks underneath us.

"Hot, isn't it?" he says.

"Shall I open the window?" I ask.

"Don't want to scandalise the neighbours."

I make him sit with his back to one of the posts, and tie his hands behind it with his own belt. He doesn't object. Then I address my mouth, my fingers, my breasts to his body. Skin against glistening, sweaty skin. The smell of him – that masculine scent that I lust after like nothing else.

8

As he did earlier to me, I worship his feet with my mouth, and he laughs, struggling to get his feet underneath himself.

"You're tickling," he accuses.

I move my mouth, finally give him what he anticipated so much earlier, my mouth around his cock, flicking and licking and sucking.

"Still tickling?" I say.

"Don't stop …"

I get him close to the edge, then move him back a pace from it before encouraging him forward to look over once more. Then, when he is very close to coming, I untie his hands and allow him free access to my body. He doesn't ask permission, but rips my blouse open with little care for the silken material. Then my bra is likewise discarded and he is feasting on my breasts until I am hot and wet and melting with desire.

At last, when he finally takes me; when we can't wait another second, he takes me over the side of the bed. I am arched back over the four-poster. Dan has one hand on each of my wrists, which are forced down into the covers. I can feel the strength of his thrusting, which is pushing me back against the mattress. It feels as if he will thrust straight through me; it feels as though that would be precisely what I want him to do. I can hear a voice crying out, and I know it is mine, yet I feel strangely divorced from it, conscious only of the feeling, the smell, the taste of sex surrounding me.

I barely know who I am any more, and certainly don't care. I remember what it felt like with his salty cock in my mouth, sliding in and out. I imagine him thrusting in my mouth with the same vigour with which he is fucking my body, and I am … I am …

He gasps, groans, shudders, and I feel him pulse inside me before the feeling is overtaken by my own climax, my own pulsating heavenly-earthy climax. We are joined in sweat and semen and lust and our cries of fulfilment battle

9

each other in the air before falling to the ground, just as he slumps down on the floor at my feet.

The silence is broken only by our gasping breaths, our thundering heartbeats. I can feel the blood pound in my head as I lie back and think of Dan, my latest but by no means my least conquest. I hear him pull himself slowly from the ground, and a second later his head is next to mine.

"You kept your promise," he remarks.

"Did you doubt me?"

"No." He pauses. "Thank you."

"For what?" I ask.

He grins at me.

"For the best fuck I've had in a long time."

He knows the rules: understood from the start that this was a one time thing. He visits the bathroom, then dresses, his jeans sliding back on, followed by the shirt and jumper. I suspect every time I see a red jumper now I will be reminded of this. As he turns toward the bedroom door I call him back.

"Dan."

"Yes?"

"Same here," I say; and with a last smile he is gone.

Captive Dove
by Alcamia

I always wanted to be a prisoner in the cage. Even as a child I wished for it. Then, I was obsessed with the huge gilded cage with the parrot, which my grandfather owned. I would press my finger to the bars and the slowly germinating sexual me demanded captivity. I soon had cages of my own as if, by collecting them, I could assuage my thirst for constraint. You see, I am an addict of imprisonment.

I have existed like this for many years, in a penumbra of morbid, sexual frustration. My lust draws me to act out strange and lurid erotic fantasies and I have discovered that without the fantasy of the cage I cannot orgasm. My dreams are haunted by images of skin caressing bar, and dripping sex within confinement, and I awake throbbing, with sex-wet sheets wrapped around my legs and arms, and my clit pulsing and unsatisfied.

I inhabit two dark rooms in a Victorian house and they are clogged with my cages. They hang from the ceiling and rest on every available surface. I have one tiny Japanese ivory cage which Takana, the boy at the oriental supermarket gave me. He said it once belonged to a Geisha, a woman with torrid sexual desires. It is so small I can hold it on my finger; inside a miniscule woman, fashioned in white, presses her cheek to the bars. I often wonder the

11

reason for that tiny cage and whether I am the only person to be so intoxicated by dreams of captivity.

Inside each of my cages I place my dolls. I am envious of their imprisonment, because they are who I want to be. Hands chained and fastened, and in various stages of undress, their captivity excites me.

I once saw a beautiful white dove in a cage on a Parisian market stall and it haunted me. Gentle yet tragic beauty fluttered in frustration against steel, but in the eyes were solace and contentment. That is how I wish to be. I want to be the captive dove.

Emile is an artist of considerable calibre and I am an artist's model. For once, I am not alone in my obsession, for Emile has so many more cages than I. He collects them like a fanatic collects art, and his art grows around them. He only ever photographs models in cages.

When I first met him, he wanted a specific bird for his cage and he chose me. I stepped into his warehouse and I was reminded of my apartment, as it was full of cages of every conceivable size and shape. It was a surreal experience to be wandering into my fantasy landscape. Instantly my dreams became stylised pastiches of depravity, woven around my captivity within Emile's art.

'You have dozens. How many do you have?'

Emile pressed his finger to his lips and smiling he rotated a cage in his hand.

'I have many hundreds. It's quite an obsession with me.'

'Where do you find them?'

'Oh! Flea markets, antique shops. People even give them to me. Artists, actors ...' He paused for effect. 'And I custom design and make them, to exacting specifications, for my art.'

'I see.' At this instant, my heart began to race and my theatre of sensuality, which is the hot, greedy sex part of me, moistened alarmingly. 'Would you ever make one for me? Perhaps for a birthday present, or because I am your perfect model? Maybe because you have fallen in love with me?' Emile did not reply and I strolled over to a cage which had quite taken my eye. 'And what about this large one? Is this for a dog?'

'No, that one belonged to a pop star. He kept a panther as a pet.'

'A panther!' My heart leapt as I crouched by the cage running my hands over the bars.

I think the cages are metaphors for Emile. Within the prison of his mind, he is as captive as am I. The cage is the manifestation of both of our warped worlds.

The other models tell me Emile is impossible to work with. Driven by an artist's mercurial temperament, no love or desire seems to stir him. Emile is entirely hidden within the cage of his psyche. However, this makes him more interesting to me and my lust for him is overpowering. I become haunted, and permanently aroused. He affects me like an illness and I am so giddy with it, I sometimes have to take a break from a photographic session to run to the bathroom and seek solitude. There, I reach my hands beneath my skirt and sink my fingers into my saturated pussy, to appease my gnawing hunger, and when I come back I reek of sex. Emile must smell the excitement clinging to my skin, as he often brushes my body. Pushing me onto the bars of the cage, as if he knows how best to inflame me. How can such a fleeting touch ignite so much passion?

Emile photographs me in many ways. Naked, in shadow. Dressed in beautiful clothes. Makeup artists transfigure me into an Egyptian princess, a nineteen twenties flapper, or tentative Eve, clad only in a thong, with my luscious breasts exposed. It is all about the cage and the mood in which he wishes to portray it. One picture became quite famous and it found its way on to the front page of a magazine. I was draped naked, over a beautiful white cage, festooned in red and white roses. Emile captured the mysterious shadows of my nipples and dark sex, and I blossomed for him. When I played with the cage, touching and entering, then stepping back, for the first time, I saw dangerous fire in his eyes and his body quivered with arousal as he fingered the bulge between his legs.

Emile is an enigma. He confuses women but he seduces few. They lust after him, but they think they fail to interest him enough and thus he tires of them quickly. It is true that he is an erudite intellectual parading his use of words and art in front of them, as if the words are a screen to the sexuality he tries to repress. But I know it is more than that. Emile wants his captive dove and I know the release of his sexuality is as dependent on bar and steel, as is my own. His artistic and intellectual sides build a wall between us, but with the cages I feel I am breaking through the thick veneer of ice that freezes his desire.

I am so easily aroused and influenced by Emile, I show him my sexuality at all times. I unbutton my blouse to expose my breasts, sitting with my skirt up high around my thighs so he catches glimpses of my shaven cunt. His equal obsession with the cages fuels my lust, making me vertiginous with need. I must be captivated by Emile and I must be his bird in the cage. No woman has ever released him, fully possessed him, and neither has a man fully possessed me. My need for imprisonment soon becomes indistinguishable from my thirst for Emile. I know the cage is as much the key to Emile's sexuality as it is my own, and all I want is to find the hidden key.

Emile watches me thoughtfully. When he is introspective his eyes become progressively darker. I enjoy staring into the twin orbs. Within them I see the world I deny myself. The first time, when he showed me the cages, he was malleable and soft. I felt I reached him through his eyes and his addictions. This is how it was, until I mentioned my desire for captivity. I am used now to his initial loosening and opening, which makes me receptive, my thighs drenched with juices, red-hot and loose. And then the closing and locking of the door to his mind in an instant. He plays me like a fish on a line. He has discovered my needs and he will build layers of seduction until he locks me in steel bondage and I explode. I look into Emile's world through the bars of his cage. A cage with bars so closely placed together, I cannot get my fingers between them. They are the bars locking away his sexuality.

Emile constructs the most complex and beautiful cages. He takes the world of his emotions and extrapolates them into the cage, as if the cages grow from his mind. He creates phantasmagorical designs of all shapes and sizes, twisted copper, lead or steel and fills them with chained lovers, contorted in grossly extrapolated poses. Yet Emile's body is imprisoned within a different kind of cage, as if the body and mind are two diametrically opposed forces.

'Your own cage is to be my latest project.' Emile says one day. 'I think I am falling in love with you, and I have a certain obsession, which I now feel ready to give birth to. You awaken things in me, Lucinda. Within you I see something which stirs my memory and deepest sexual fantasies. I see, in you, the eroticism of captivity.

He draws me down beside him and his mouth and tongue dance over my lips. I sit breathless, hardly daring to move. I experience the heat from his body, burning my hands and searing my snatch, and I quiver and tremble with virgin-like excitement.

'Once!' he continues, 'when I was in Buenos Aires, I visited this club and I saw a woman dancing in a cage. I cannot explain the beauty of this woman. Her limbs were naked and she shone from the oil she rubbed onto her skin. Every night I went back to the club, and she drew the dark sensuality out of me. She was my artistic muse. I fell in love with her. But only, you understand, in the cage. She was my captive dove. There was no dancer in all of Buenos Aires like her. She said the captivity made her so sensual, because it unlocked her deepest desires and it excited her. She loved men's eyes on her body. When she danced, her cunt poured like a faucet, the droplets running down her thighs. The more the men stared, the more excited she became. Her hips would thrust and she ejaculated just like a man. I never saw anything quite so erotic. Then she would lean through the bars and say, 'Emile, I love you.' One day she gave up dancing in the cage, as she knew other men looking at her upset me. I said to her you were good in it, I liked and admired the beauty of you very much inside the cage, why did you have to fly free? You see, she had got it very wrong. Yes, I was a little jealous, but when she left the cage it killed my fascination, as she became someone else entirely. She didn't understand. After that she became angry, she went away.'

I did not know how to respond to this. For a while I felt jealous of the woman in the cage. She'd captured Emile's love and it was something I craved. Somehow she had turned the key.

'Why do you wish to be captive, Lucinda? Is it because you want to be a prisoner to your own fantasies, or simply submissive? You are a strong, independent woman. Do you crave a man to master you? Why else would you be drawn to a metal cube?'

'All of that.' I poke out my tongue to caress his. 'All of that and much more. The cage unlocks my sexuality. It is the key to who I am.'

Actually, I am so excited at the thought of the cage, because it is being formed from the complexity of my love of Emile's mind. It is as if my cage is an extension of his art, body and penis.

On the day he gives me the gift of the cage, he brings me to the warehouse and gently removes the blindfold he has placed over my eyes. 'You see each bar is painted alternately black and white, to reflect the dark and light sides of your sexuality. I had to place you in a palace of

16

towering cupolas and minarets. You are to be my caged Goddess.'

I almost faint from orgasmic arousal. Emile holds me, vibrating, as I respond to his constant teasing of my nipples. I stare at the cage, and, like the exotic Buenos Aires woman, I ooze fluids.

Emile observes me, his tongue occasionally flicking out to lick at his sensual lips.

'You are an apple gone bad, aren't you, Lucinda? I was attracted to you instantly. I saw in you someone the same as myself; a pure clean dove with dirtied wings. A creature of captive desires.' He touches my lip with his finger and I take it into my mouth, sucking hungrily. It is as if the cage draws all the energy from my body. It enslaves me. I run forward and let my tongue press the bars. I tear open my buttons and grind my naked flesh against it.

'Emile. Put me inside. I want to be your captive dove now.' I whisper seductively, blowing my breath onto his lips. 'Darling. I don't often beg for something do I? Kiss me and lock me in the cage. I know it excites you as much as it does me.'

I have never wanted a man like I want Emile. But he plays with me. He hooks me with his perverse needs and now he winds in the line slowly. He will not seduce me, he enjoys gently tantalising me, and I am now feeling aggressive from my sexual need.

'You're afraid that, if you unlock that part of you, it won't get back in its cage.' I once said of his emotions. Yet, your art is all about the cages.'

Emile fondles me and a delicious shiver explodes across the surface of my skin. He is able to awaken me immediately. His sexual energy is so magnetic, it wraps around me like invisible thread, squeezing my nipples into tight buds and forcing my cunt fountain, to flow.

'Beg me, Lucinda. Say, Emile I beg you to lock me in

the cage.' He grips my chin and stares into my eyes. 'I know what you want. I know the cage is the manifestation of your warped fantasies.'

I wait for his kiss. Yet even as he brushes my lips with his, I know he won't take me. He flicks his tongue out to trace the outline of my mouth and my body erupts in orgasmic flame. 'Put me inside it now.'

'You must beg me. On your hands and knees, Lucinda.'

Emile slides his hand under my blouse and I place my palms on to his bare skin. Then, I tease his naked nipples. I love the rigid points, primed with lust. I want to lick and taste them, drive Emile to the brink of delirious pleasure. But only within the cage. I drop onto my knees and I look up imploringly. 'I beg you. Lock me in the cage.'

Emile takes the tiny key from around his neck and he unlocks the door. I step inside. I touch devices designed for restraint. Manacle, chain, rope, even the swing designed for a human bird. Within the crepuscular shadows of the warehouse, the light dances on the bars of my prison.

My nipples tighten and I feel the familiar heat between my legs. Emile comes up behind me and his hands brush my blouse. Next he eases his finger beneath the buttons and his hand grips my breasts. My body becomes a roaring, fluid rush. Every muscle and fibre of my pussy loosening and contracting in spasms of tetany, as Emile presses my body against the bars of the cage. The cage will untie me, free me.

Then, he pushes me inside and locking the gate, he hangs the key around his neck. 'Now I shall leave you for a while, Lucinda. I will give you time to discover your gift. Certainly, I will come back. You won't know when of course. However, I will return to feed you. Perhaps to play with you. You would like that, wouldn't you?'

'Oh yes, Emile!' I whisper breathlessly, gripping and sliding my fingers up and down the gilded bars. Pressing my lipstick drenched mouth to the steel. 'I adore the cage.

Emile. Thank you so much.'

Will he starve me, play with me. Seduce me? Will I writhe at the feet of my captor, begging for freedom and sexual release? My body resonates with primal lust.

I undress. I unbutton my blouse and unzip my skirt. Next I wriggle out of my silk panties and kick off my high heels. Then I press my limbs against the bars; thigh, breast, and cheek, rubbing cat-like on them, as I feel my sex pulse rise. I let the bars imprint nipple and burning clit, groaning as I orgasm in rapid convulsions.

After a while I sit down on the steel floor, enjoying the cooling sensation of steel on super-heated sex. I adore Emile because he has made my dream come true. I always knew his liberated spirit could create the magnificent cage which would unlock me.

I crawl around the floor, like a human panther, leaving a snail-like blossom of sex desire behind me. I gaze at the small swing, swaying gently and I remember the woman in the cage and how Emile said she would hang upside down, displaying her large pendulous breasts and gaping, shaved pussy. Yet the woman in the cage blew her chances with Emile and I intend not to. Within my private prison of delight, furnished with toys and ropes provided by my captor, I intend to seduce Emile. I will be his captive dove.

Using my muscular arms to lift myself onto the swing, I sit there, rocking gently to and fro. Emile loves the agility of my curvaceous body. Then, I part my legs over the steel swing and I purr with delight as it slips between my saturated cleft. I flex and contract my pelvic muscles around it, pumping rhythmically up and down, as I imagine Emile's dextrous fingers and sinuous cock ramming in and out of my snatch. Satiated, I lower myself to the floor, drawing up my knees to my chin. And between the curves of my thighs, the pursed lips of my cunt pucker, in readiness for the kiss of Emile's cock.

Soon I become a little bored and I call. 'Emile, I need

you. Why don't you come to me?' My fists tighten around the bars. I am aware now of the acuteness of my senses and the gnawing hunger of lust. There is a timelessness within the cage. In the silence I hear the rattle of wind on the corrugated roof, and the ebb and flow of my own aroused breath, as I dream of Emile. Seconds extend and my dreams of sex elongate with them, it is all I can think about. Bored, my hands cup my breasts, invigorating and pinching my nipples until they are red and rigid. Gradually, my hands insinuate themselves between my thighs and I lay writhing on the floor of the cage, my fingers dancing and slipping in and out of my hungry red maw and around the engorged tip of clit and sucking hole. I climax in a frenzy of gasps and bucking hips, and then I lay still.

Still my arousal grows. I need new ways to appease myself. I spread-eagle my legs and push them through the bars. I press my labia and clit against them as closely as I can in an intimate embrace. I grind and wriggle. My need now to urinate inflames me, until I orgasm again, with such ferocious intensity, I almost faint. When I collapse on the floor of the cage, I am branded with streaks from the bars of the cage.

I am so feverish with my need for Emile, I do not know what to do with myself next. I toss and turn, I lay on belly and back and I spread out my arms and legs in a star, laying in a state of abandon dreaming of Emile. Later I prowl the cage, like the captive panther, twisting and purring. My feline eyes searching the shadows. 'You bastard! Emile. How dare you leave me so long! I hope you're satisfied.' Yet my anger commingles with something more potent, the germinating dark side of a hidden and fierce sensuality.

I must have fallen asleep because I awaken to Emile, who is fastening a collar around my neck and manacles to my wrists. He has taken my clothes and thrown them outside the cage. Instead of anger I experience intense sexual fire. He says nothing, he simply strokes my cheek

20

and then he locks the door. 'Emile, bring back my clothes.' I rattle the bars of the cage angrily.

Once more I clamber onto the swing. But, this time, I allow it to gain momentum, until I am soaring, and as close as I can be to the sides of the cage. With one hand I reach out and grab the bars, and, swinging monkey-like, I release the swing and grasp them, clutching like a limpet to my prison. I am higher than I thought and I can see most of the warehouse. I am hoping Emile is hidden and observing me. 'Emile, you rat, come and let me out.'

When Emile finally returns, I am startled to see he is already naked. He clips a chain to the collar and he draws me tightly against the bars. I close my eyes. I enjoy the sense of him being close in velvet darkness, his eyes stroking my skin.

'You must be hungry by now, Lucinda,' Emile says, rolling a peach into the cage. I pounce on it, making a great performance of sitting with my legs spread wide, through the bars, exposing my labia, while I suck on the juicy flesh.

Tightening the chain Emile pulls my face to steel, and as he kisses my peach-wet lips, I feel his wet penis graze my maw. 'Shall I release you now, or will I wait? Perhaps I will keep you here for ever, my captive dove? I would never tire of watching you.' He cups my buttocks and my pussy pouts forward to taste him. The tip of the engorged cock teases, enters and recedes. Emile pushes the door open gently with his finger. 'You could have left the cage whenever you wanted. You never even tried it, to see if it were locked. That's because part of you never wanted to leave the cage, did it, Lucinda? Even now you will not leave.' Emile enters the cage. He locks the door and then holding up the key he throws it through the bars.

'You fool what did you do that for? How do we get out of here? Ah! You are still playing and the door is still open. You are engaging me in a psychological game.'

'That is for you to find out, darling.' Emile laughs,

gripping the chain and pinning me to the floor, his monstrous cock grazing my greedy flesh. I bite and suck at his skin in paroxysms of pleasure.

'What do you think will happen?' He whispers in my ear. 'Do you think we will die in here?'

I think of the dove beating its wings against the bars of the cage and my sex drips nectar. Emile devours my mouth, breast and cunt, and his cock pushes inside my warm cave. Cock and mouth enter and return until the cock, inflamed and distended by Emile's captivity, begins its rumbustious pumping into and out of my sex-wet, lubricious tunnel. 'I love you Emile.'

I am Emile's captive dove and in its turn the cage has unlocked Emile.

Wash And Blow Job
by Les Hansom

Tim needed a haircut. Tim needed a lot of things, but at the moment his wife had decided that he needed a haircut. His wife decided lots of things. His wife had decided that Tim should have a vasectomy, just as easily as she had decided that he would not go out on his mate's stag night this evening, and that he was going to grout the bathroom when his hair had been cut – in a salon of her choosing, that she had booked on his behalf. His wife stopped him going to the smoky old barber shop in town because the men talked about women all the time and what they would do with them given the chance. Not only that, there were pornographic magazines in the barber shop. Of course by pornography she meant those national papers that printed pictures of naked women; basically, anything that could potentially give Tim a hard-on. What her problem was with Tim getting a stiffy was unknown. Maybe she was put on earth to torture him. But, whatever the case, she certainly didn't oblige him herself.

The salon was in the centre of town above a shop that sold clothes. He saw the sign outside – Trim – and climbed the stairs inside. He briefly considered the connotations of the salon's name and chuckled to himself as he opened the door.

"Private joke?" said a cheerful voice, catching him off-guard as he entered.

He looked up, startled, and saw a young girl, about twenty years old, smiling at him from behind a small counter. She had shoulder-length, curly blonde hair, tanned skin and little or no make-up at all. This girl didn't need it, she was naturally beautiful. Her face instantly cheered him up, and the prospect of getting his haircut didn't look so bad after all.

"Hi," he said, "no, I was just thinking of a programme I watched last night."

"Do you have an appointment, Mr …?"

"Young," he replied, "Mr Young."

"Oh yes, I see here. Only this says Mrs Young," she looked at him and smiled, "did your wife make the appointment for you?"

"Yeah … erm, I didn't have time to. That's right, sorry," replied Tim a little too self-consciously.

"Doesn't matter to me who makes the appointment, Mr Young," she said.

"Please, call me Tim, are you cutting my hair?" he asked.

"I am a hairdresser, Tim, and I'm the only one here. Come on over and take a seat."

Tim followed her over to one of those backward sinks. He didn't realise that his wife had booked him in for a wash also. The sinks made him nervous. He'd read somewhere that they could trap nerves in your neck when you bent over them backwards. He did the British thing and went along with it anyway.

"Make yourself comfortable, Tim, and I'll be back in just a second." She started to walk away and then stopped and turned towards him, "I'm Jessica, by the way."

Tim sat in the chair and leaned back. He was surprised because the sink had a cushion under his neck; it felt quite comfortable. When Jessica returned he noticed that she had removed her cardigan. She had exposed some flesh and she looked very nice indeed. She was wearing shorts just like Tim, with the pockets all over them, the ones that are so far down your leg that you put your back out trying to get your wallet. On top she was wearing a low-cut yellow vest top. Tim raised his head a little and looked at her pert little tits. She was not wearing a bra either. He put his head back down and sighed to himself. 'If only I were a little younger,' he thought.

"Right then," said Jessica, leaning over him from the side, "lets get you all wet shall we?"

Tim rolled his eyes into the bottom of their sockets, straining to look down her top. She caught his eye and smiled. "Well," said Tim randomly, pretending not to notice her smile, "I didn't realise I was booked in for a wash?" he enquired.

"You're not," she said casually, "but it's the end of the day and you're my last customer. I thought I'd treat you a little, you look like you deserve it."

Tim was amazed. "Well, thanks. But, you don't have …"

"Enough now, just relax. If I didn't want to, believe me I wouldn't."

Tim did exactly that. He closed his eyes and watched the light change as she moved her arms over him. He wanted to moan with pleasure when he felt the warm water run through his hair. As Jessica moved over him, stretching to the back of his head, he caught the smell of her perfume in the air, and mixed with the shampoo she was using, he fell under the spell of her strange pheromone and almost swooned. The skin of her wrists brushed across his forehead. She felt very delicate, like she might break if she rubbed the shampoo in too hard. He had an overwhelming urge to sit up and hold her tight. He could feel a stirring in his shorts. His wife certainly would not agree with this, but how could she have guessed that washing his hair would give him an erection?

"All done, now just sit still and I'll wrap a towel around

25

your head," she said.

They moved over to a chair by the window. It was beginning to get dark and the street lights had just been turned on.

"What time is it please?" asked Tim.

"It's a little after 5.30," answered Jessica, closing the blinds near the mirror, "I'm just going to put the closed sign up and lock the door. Back in a two shakes of a lamb's tail."

Tim watched her lamb's tail walk away in the reflection of the mirror. It had that lovely little swaying motion that all the best asses have, moving up, down, and side to side like a slow waltz in her shorts. Tim's cock twitched again. He reached under the waistband of his shorts and found it. He gave it a little squeeze to try and get it down, but alas it did not work; he only excited it more. He tried trapping the end under his waistband also, but that didn't work either. Facing facts, Tim knew he just had to make sure that the smock she had placed over him did not droop down onto his groin area, otherwise he would make the whole thing look like a poorly constructed tent. Jessica returned, switching off some of the background lights on her way. There were only a few remaining and when she walked into the primary light over Tim's mirror she looked amazing. She had tied up her shoulder-length curls into a kind of pony-tail. What Tim liked about it was that he could get a good look at her face. She had a big, almost simian, jaw and mouth, a little like Billy Piper's, the type that protrudes further than the other facial features in profile, and the type that Tim just wanted to stick his cock into. She stood behind him and took his hair in her hands, gently stroking it between her fingers.

"You have lovely hair, Tim," she said, "what are we going to do with it then?"

"Just a bit of a trim," he answered, remembering the name of the place and trying not to laugh out loud. He smiled to himself.

"Something amusing?" asked Jessica.

"Just the name of the place, you know."

"No?" said Jessica in an enquiring tone, "what about it?"

"Have you never heard the expression 'a bit of trim'?" asked Tim

"Oh I get it, yeah." she said, "but it's not that funny is it?"

"I think it's generational Jessica. Your lot don't use it much nowadays."

"So am I a bit of trim, Tim?" she laughed at the rhyme.

Tim joined her. "Oh yes!" he said, getting carried away, "you certainly are."

Tim immediately reddened. He had loosened up a little too much and was pretty embarrassed at what he had said. Jessica saw this and rescued him.

"Right, one trim coming up."

They hardly spoke at all for a long time, and Jessica worked slowly and carefully, lifting his hair in her fingers and measuring the length before each cut of the scissors. Tim liked it best when she walked around the front of him and put her hands either side of his head, gently pulling at his hair to check the symmetry of the cut. She was at eye level with him, but not looking at his eyes. He was looking at her though. He felt as though he was behind a one-way mirror and Jessica was oblivious to his presence. They were so close he could feel her breath on the tip of his nose. He looked a little further down and saw her pert little breasts standing up despite her stooping. Her top was so low cut that he could see everything. This gave him an enormous hard-on; so hard it hurt him to stay in the same position. He began to wriggle around.

"Are you alright, Tim?" asked Jessica, concerned about his awkward movements.

"Yes, I'm sorry, I'm a little itchy with the hair."

"Let me get my brush."

Jessica reached for a soft neck brush and dashed it across

Tim's neck and face. Tim sneezed and Jessica dropped the brush in his lap. This little twist of fate revealed Tim's secret, and created the poorly constructed tent he was so worried about. Jessica reached for the brush, pretending to ignore the huge erection coming out of the black smock. She failed to disguise her longing though because Tim saw her in the mirror. Jessica moved around behind him again and tried to concentrate on the haircut. She was getting hot, Tim could see sweat on her brow. He was getting pretty hot also in the smock, and the fact that he was sitting in front of a beautiful girl he would love to screw, with a hard-on the size of a king size Toblerone, did not help matters.

"So what do you do, Tim," asked Jessica, virtually salivating and looking down at his cock between scissor snips.

"I'm in demolition," said Tim nervously. What he wanted to say of course was, 'Get my cock out now before it snaps under the pressure'.

"What do *you* do exactly?" she asked.

"I get to blow shit up. It's the perfect job for a bloke," he laughed. His cock was beginning to slacken a little as he felt a conversation beginning.

"I like to blow sometimes too. And it's the perfect job for a woman," Jessica laughed out loud. Tim's cock twitched again and he laughed out loud with her. "Some people like that, and some don't. I suppose it's a matter of taste," she laughed.

"And *how* you taste," Tim chipped in.

They both laughed again and looked at each other in the mirror. Tim stifled his laugh when he caught Jessica's eye.

"How *do you* taste, Tim?" she said, looking very serious for a moment.

"Pardon?" said Tim, not quite believing what he had just heard.

"I want to know what you taste like?"

"I … I don't know," he stammered, a little confused at

the direction these minor flirtations were taking, "I don't get much chance to taste myself," he laughed nervously, trying desperately to make light of an obvious proposition.

"Mind if I find out?" said Jessica, already bending to her knees.

"Are you crazy!" exclaimed Tim. "No, of course I don't. I mean, I don't … no thank you. Please stop."

"Does your wife do this?" she said, ignoring Tim's mindless, and frankly unconvincing, pleas.

On her knees, looking up at him, she slid her hand up the inside leg of his shorts, forcing him to quiver as she approached his groin area. Tim didn't move a muscle. This felt fantastic, and there was no way he would protest any longer. This girl was right, why not enjoy himself. She found her way to his boxers and without any further warning she put her hand up the leg of them and found his cock, nice and hard and bursting to get out.

"Oh yeah," she said, raising her eyebrows, "can I taste some of that, Tim?"

"If you don't get it out soon, I will," he replied, surprising himself with his newfound confidence.

Jessica threw back the smock and it covered Tim's face. She wrestled frantically with the buttons on his shorts as he wrestled with the smock over his face. When he finally saw what was going on he gazed in awe at the creature between his legs. Jessica looked fantastic. She had taken off her top, revealing those beautiful tits he had been peeking at and she was working on springing his cock from its joyless prison. Jessica grinned at him hungrily and popped the swollen end of his cock into her mouth. She had a tight grip with her hand on the base and it felt wonderful. He watched her head move from side to side as she circled the end in her wet mouth. He moaned out loud as he felt twitching around his asshole.

"Is this a special treat or what?" asked Jessica, coming up briefly for air and smiling at him.

29

"Hell yes!" he replied, "suck it baby."

Jessica did not disappoint. She opened that wide mouth of hers as far as it would go and shook his cock from its base, letting it bang and twitch around her lips and tongue. She wanked it hard and fast while she did this, and Tim's legs began to twitch.

"Hit a nerve I think," laughed Jessica, barely audible with her mouth full of Tim's cock.

Tim tensed his ass and legs, pointing his toes. His wanted to cum so much he was starting to get a headache.

"Relax, will you," said Jessica, taking his cock out and stroking it gently in her hand, "I'll make you cum baby, you don't need to help me."

"Right, OK," said Tim, a little shakily.

Jessica put his cock between her lips and pressed them together tight. She looked him in the eye and moved her mouth, wobbling her chin up and down quickly to make lots of saliva. She allowed a little of it to creep around her grip on his cock and slid her head down slowly, still looking at him. She continued until she had the whole thing in her mouth. She was so totally relaxed with his cock so far inside her mouth that Tim couldn't believe his eyes. She was still looking at him with innocent-looking puppy eyes, as if asking him not to hurt her. His cock started to twitch uncontrollably inside her mouth, but she did not let go of her grip, she just nuzzled a little further into his pubic hair at the base.

"Oh my God! That's fantastic," he exclaimed.

There was a surprised sound from Jessica as though she were enquiring if what he said was really true. The vibrations from the back of her throat when she did this made Tim's cock tingle with pleasure and twitch harder than ever. Jessica started to make sniggering sounds, like she was struggling to breathe through her nose, and it was quite clear that she needed to come up for air. She slid her beautiful big mouth back up Tim's length and let his cock end out of her vice-like grip with an audible 'pop' sound. She gasped and smiled all at the same time, it was quite a sight for Tim.

"You want to cum baby?" she said, "I'm only charging for the haircut."

"I want to cum so bad I could do it just looking at you," he replied.

Jessica smiled, clearly flattered, and slid back down his cock again. This time she did not stay at the base, she slid up and down the entire length and every time she went right down Tim groaned out loud. He glanced up at himself in the mirror. He looked flushed, and his nostrils were flaring like a dragon about to breathe fire. He looked down to check the reality of the situation and found Jessica sucking him off faster and faster, still taking the whole length of him inside. She had remembered how he liked it when she made noises so she did it again. Her gentle moans while sucking his cock made Tim go crazy, the vibrations were like tremors of pleasure, rattling right down into his balls. He began to gasp and tense himself.

"Ready?" said Jessica in a muffled, semi-audible voice.

"Now baby, now!" shouted Tim, as he tried to pull his cock away from her.

Jessica gave one last long slide down his length and made Tim cum a little in her mouth before pulling it out and pointing it straight ahead. She gripped the base of his cock tight as it throbbed with all the pumping. When she released her grip, Tim sprayed a long stream of cum as far as the mirror, running onto the shelf and across the floor, onto Jessica's hand. He looked up at himself and found that he had exploded all over his reflection in the mirror, in particular around the mouth.

"There," said Jessica, rising to her feet, smiling and pointing at the mirror, "now you *can* taste yourself."

Jessica moved around the back of Tim's head and held up the mirror, "Well?" she asked, "is that alright for you, sir?"

"Sure, that's great!" said Tim, tucking his cock back in his shorts, "the wife will be well pleased."

Running Free
by Beverly Langland

It is difficult to describe how it happened, how I, Alex, outwardly meek-looking, quiet and unassuming, so blatantly broke the law. Of course, it wasn't a conscious decision on my part and I still don't fully understand why the Park Ranger deemed it necessary to detain me for so long. After all, I had harmed no one. Although, I suppose darting from car to car naked gave him some justification, or maybe I should say incentive. Still, he was kind enough to loan me a blanket, kind enough to offer compassion when I failed utterly to justify my exhibitionism, kind enough to pretend not to notice the aura of sex enveloping me.

To be honest, I never intended to go into the park. Despite what the Ranger might have suspected I hadn't gone looking for anonymous sex. He grinned as he made notes of my lame excuses. Or was it a smirk? I was too embarrassed to look closely. If I had I might have noted that the glint in his eye was a little more than amusement. He had every right to be cautious for I discovered later that I had chosen a notorious spot for certain 'nocturnal activities' for my private rebellion.

On impulse, I had pulled the car into the picnic area. I felt too stressed, too uptight to go home, felt perhaps a walk would help, would ease the tension. At least I could stretch my legs. After the long overnight drive from my parents' ranch I needed to ease my cramped muscles, to clear my mind. Though, as soon as I cut the engine, a peculiar shiver ran down my spine. A deathly silence hung heavy in the morning air and at first I found the quiet a little unnerving. That early in the morning the picnic area was deserted. For a time I just sat at one of the wooden picnic benches, staring into the cold grey light of morning. Then I decided to hang around for the sun to rise. Why not? I had no reason to hurry. Without the children, there was no one waiting to welcome me. Truth was, I felt reluctant to face the emptiness.

I slipped off my shoes, letting the cool morning air soothe my aching flesh. I've always preferred walking in bare feet. Wearing shoes for hours on end didn't seem natural to me. I knew that not too far back in my ancestry lay a trace of native blood, though my uptight in-laws refused to acknowledge any such heritage. Although one only had to look at me to recognize the truth. I have dark skin, high cheekbones, straight black hair. My parents affectionately consider me a throwback. Though our family origins are almost forgotten. Conveniently so. Only Great Grandmother still mumbled the old stories – tales, which had captivated me as a child. Tales of White Feather and the six giants. Tales of other heroes and heroines. My favourite, the story of the enchanted moccasins.

Closing my eyes, I tried to recall the details of Little Doe's fables, tried to recapture the sense of belonging I once discovered there, in the wilderness. I recalled camping trips to the great forest, skinny-dipping in the lakes with the other children, running naked, running free. How long ago those days seemed, how far away happiness. Oh, to be young and carefree again!

Of course, the great forest was wilderness no longer. It had been encroached on so often the woodland was barely a fraction of its original size, though its range remained sufficiently great for unwary travellers to become lost. Few came to the forest, now. Fewer still ventured past the picnic areas and nature reserves.

I yawned, stretched. Slowly the sun crept above the tree line, bathing me in glorious sunshine. The warmth was wonderful, therapeutic. As the heat penetrated deeper, I felt a weight lift from my shoulders. Then, for no apparent reason other than a sudden feeling of childlike adventure I removed my blouse, exposed my skin to the sun's healing rays. I felt as if some invisible shackle had been unlocked. I glimpsed a sudden image of freedom. Looking around cautiously at the deserted picnic tables I removed my bra, let my breasts swing free. Another impulsive action. I decided I liked that, liked the notion that I *still* could be impulsive. After the drudgery of the long drive it felt sensuous also to feel the morning breeze wash over me, to feel the tender kiss of cool air tease my nipples. Already they were hard stubs, increasing my sense of playfulness.

Emboldened, I stepped from the seating terrace onto the lawn-like clearing, now awash with sunlight, feeling the dew beneath my skin, the clinging grass between my toes. The cool dampness felt soothing under my feet, the warmth of the sun wonderful on my shoulders, my back, and my breasts. I looked skywards towards the glorious orb, spotted the Moon still lingering in the sky. I held out my hands. What a day! Even the trees were rejoicing. They shimmered in the breeze, reflecting the muted greens of morning. I felt suddenly alive and ageless. Like an impetuous child I twirled and danced, arms outstretched, whooping and giggling, embracing the day. Then – again on a whim, or perhaps by then I was conniving – I removed my panties. I no longer wanted them. They were old, stuffy, not right for a child of nature. I threw them into a litterbin. Feeling wicked I twirled again, spinning faster and faster, my light summer skirt rising high above my waist, cool air rushing between my thighs. I heard a car approach but did not care.

I kept spinning. Spun until the trees blurred, until I fell to the ground – giddy and intoxicated.

For a time I lay still, waiting while my vision returned, watching the leaves as they grew gradually lighter. I lay passively with wide eyes as the last vestiges of night turned into day. As one realm bowed out to the next, an owl hooted its presence – an age-old ritual of the passing. For some reason I felt drawn to the sound. Moving nearer to the edge of the forest, I peered longingly into its mysterious depths. The trail looked old, forgotten, dark and a little threatening. However, the long rays of the sun shone bright, forced their way between the branches, like a beacon showing me the way, urging me forward.

Intrigued, I edged past the tree line, edged deeper into the woods. Soon, the soft grass beneath my feet gave way to tree bark, to moss, to imagined insects wriggling between my toes. I felt connected to the soft earth, more connected there than to the bricks and mortar I foolishly still called home. As I delved deeper, my sense of belonging grew strong, the lure of the wood overpowering my underlying sense of trepidation. I felt empowered, felt a strong compulsion to venture further, to lose myself within the multitude of trees. I looked skyward through the canopy of leaves, spotted the moon again. She kept watch over me so I pressed on.

When I eventually looked over my shoulder, I could no longer see the edge of the wood nor the picnic area. Surrounded by trees the way ahead seemed much darker, but I was not afraid. High above in the treetops the owl hooted again; marking the end of his watch, calling to me from deep inside the forest, reminding me that I was not alone. I followed his call at a brisk walk, skipping as a child set free after school.

Then, with no conscious decision to do so, I broke into a trot, then a canter. God, I couldn't remember the last time I had run for the sake of running, for the pleasure alone and not from fear. Such pleasure, such freedom! Suddenly even my delicate skirt became too restrictive. I wanted to be free. Totally free. I tore at the flimsy material, cast the ruins aside without breaking stride, without a second thought of the consequence of my action. Once in nature's garb, the chill forest air enveloped me completely. Goose-pimples invaded my skin despite the heat of my exertion. Invigorated, I ran ...

Ran like only a child can when first she discovers the power in her legs, the exhilarating thrill pushing her to the limit of control. I felt amazed how surefooted my control after all these years. Exalted with my strength, my power, I ran ...

Ran as if the wind itself hounded me, my long lithe legs eating the distance with easy, confident strides. Somehow I kept running. Even when the brush grew thick, even when thorny bushes barred my way, when vines and ivy stuck long tendrils into my path. I ran. Occasionally, the point of a branch would nick my skin; lash me as I barged forward. Still, I ran on, offering only an occasional wince from the whiplash of a twig or the jar of a loose stone under the sole of my feet.

As I ran I felt a change within me, felt an inner self break free, drawing me ever closer to Mother Nature. The call of the wild grew overwhelming. I rushed onward, now with a keen sense of anticipation. I felt at peace with myself, with the forest, with the world at large. As my sense of peace grew so did my strength. Soon I found myself bounding over fallen branches with ease. I absorbed the sights, sounds, smells of the woodland I passed. I became aware of other woodland animals hiding, cowering in the thick undergrowth, scampering for cover as I invaded their space. In my mind, I became mistress of the forest, felt invigorated by the control surging through me. High on adrenaline and now aroused I ran ...

Ran until I felt my pounding heart would burst. Ran until

my lungs grew rasping raw from the effort. Ran until my oxygen-starved muscles cried out in pain. Ran until the heartbroken woman, the browbeaten housewife existed no more, until I became whole again. A woman once more. Only then did I slow, when the pain grew too great, when its pureness washed clear all other feeling other than the primitive arousal surging through my loins. Still I tried, soaking up the pain, letting out the hurt until I could no longer remember why I cried each night. Only then did I stop, pausing for breath in a shady glade. I sank to the ground, back resting against an ancient tree. I felt so alive!

I lifted my knees, parted my legs. I could smell my excitement. I touched my engorged pussy, feeling the fierce heat there, the sopping wetness. I deliberately, wantonly spread my legs wider. I didn't want to feel ashamed for what I intended to do. I had hidden under the duvet for too long. Now I wanted to expose my longing. I no longer had a husband, any man for that matter. So what! Abstinence wasn't a crime whatever Mother implied. I was tired of playing by other people's rules, of unsuitable dates, of unsuitable men with unsuitable appetites. I wasn't ready to let another man into my life. My mind was suddenly clear. It was OK to be alone, to be independent.

My sex ached for release, moist with the slickness of my juices; my animal scent filled the clearing, the musky aroma turning me on more. I had another courtship to play, a much simpler more earthy ritual. I tentatively touched my clitoris, gasped with delight as it sprang instantly to life. With one finger I traced little circles around the sensitive nub, my other hand roaming urgently over my body while the diligent finger worked its magic. Rolling onto one buttock, I caressed my hips and buttocks, explored the crease between the cheeks, fingering, rubbing the skin between anus and sex. This is a sensitive spot for me, and there I wasn't embarrassed to rejoice in the delightful feeling, occasionally spreading my wetness so I could slip a fingertip past my sphincter.

Once more supine, I spread my legs, ran my palms along the quivering inside of my thighs, then over my pouting sex, caressing my belly, my navel, my breasts, happy that I could fondle my body so freely, so openly. As I curled fingertips into my unfolding sex, I closed my eyes, tried desperately not to think of Jeremy. Tried not to remember how he used to touch me, how his hard, living flesh penetrated me so readily. Oh, how I loved the feel of him, so big, so hard, claiming me for his own. I forced the image of a naked Jeremy from my mind, tried to drag someone else, anyone, into my fantasy without success.

Frustrated, I opened my eyes and gasped in surprise. Watching cautiously from the far side of the clearing stood a great elk, his dark eyes questioning, challenging. He was a bull of a beast. I could make out his powerful muscles rippling beneath his beautiful coat, magnificent antlers crowning his broad head. I had never seen an elk up close before. I thought the animal an omen of some kind. Perhaps this majestic king of the forest had come to claim me, to take me away from all I hated. Despite the creature's size, I didn't feel frightened. Apprehensive maybe, though strangely my apprehension only fuelled my excitement. I probed deeper into my wetness, pushing two fingers as far as I could manage, all the while staring into the elk's demanding brown orbs through half-lidded eyes. For some reason I wanted to do this most natural of deeds, wanted to pleasure myself in the elk's domain, to challenge his authority. As I slowly fingered myself, the elk took a tentative step closer. I willed the beast forward and when the elk took another step, I imagined him magically transformed into a primitive native warrior.

I closed my eyes. The elk-man came to me then, took me in his tree-like arms, and gently lowered me onto his impossibly large erection. I took him easily, my unbelievable wetness easing my descent until he had me fully impaled. I exalted in the way he filled me. Not just my cunt but my whole being. The elk-man too cried out with delight. He backed me against the rough bark of the ancient tree, slowly, yet forcibly drove himself deeper still. I felt crushed between the two forces of nature. Knew then the strength I had felt was nothing compared with his. So I gave myself to him. I clung to the elk-man, digging my nails deep, fearing he would let me fall and the forest would claim me as one of its own.

He didn't. Nor did he heed my whimpers as he savagely pumped into me, wildly rutting his way to release. He was all animal. All instinct. All beast. He showed no discernable emotion towards me as a woman. He made no attempt to kiss, no attempt to seduce. He used me as wild beasts use the female. Only a few harsh grunts passed his lips as he callously pinned me against the tree. That suited me fine. I felt in no mood for romance, in no mood for love or unnecessary complication. All I needed was for elk-man to fill the void deep in the pit of my being – to fuck life back into me. I wrapped my aching legs around his waist, drawing him deeper, encouraging him to break through the barrier of hurt.

Inspired by my goading, the elk-man broke into a final frenzy of action. I didn't mind the discomfort. I felt wonderfully alive. Felt wanted. Felt needed. Soon I felt no distress at all, only an all-consuming fire signalling nature's ultimate victory. For a moment we were one, shared the same urgency, the same quest for life. Then having shown me my weakness, I showed the elk-man my strength. As he came gushing inside me – the instant of his vulnerability – I took control, rode him to my own wonderful climax, milking every last drop of life-force from his body. I kept riding and riding until I felt too sore to continue, until I lay spent and exhausted in his arms. Then, close to collapse, he gently set my trembling body onto the soft moss.

I eventually opened my eyes, smiled at the elk who watched still from the edge of the clearing. The great beast lowered his head, a bow perhaps in silent gratitude to his mate. Sated, he turned, and then disappeared into the dark thicket of trees. I marvelled at how real my fantasy had felt. Never before had masturbation satisfied me so thoroughly, never before had my fingers so completely filled me. Drained, I felt myself lulled into a blissfully sleep.

When I awoke the sun sat high in the sky, the moon finally put to bed. I knew I should move, yet I felt reluctant to leave the clearing. Somehow, I had to retrieve my clothes from the picnic terrace, get back to my car unseen. Surprisingly, I held no apprehension of someone finding me strolling naked through the forest. Only when I approached the road and the threat of civilisation did I become a little nervous. Slipping past the picnic spot turned out to be easier than I imagined. The few people visiting the nature reserve that day were too self-involved to notice me, though I had to abandon any idea of salvaging my clothes. It was only in the car park that I had the altercation with the Park Ranger. After much pleading, he let me off with a warning, with a promise not to repeat my misdemeanour. Though I had to smile when sitting in his pick-up with only a blanket for modesty, he offered me his card. He looked nice, sincere, so I took it. Who knows, perhaps I was ready to move on after all?

During the drive home, I vowed to visit the forest again. Maybe the following weekend once Jeremy had collected the children. I knew seeing him would make me uptight, make me tense. Jeremy had an uncanny knack of riling me, of bringing on a migraine by his presence alone. Despite my promise to the Ranger a run through the wilderness would do me good, would boost my self-esteem. There, I could unshackle the chains of conventionality, relieve the demands of single parenthood – truly become a free spirit if only for a short time. Yes, I would lose Alex in the woods, don a new persona.

From that moment on, in that place, I would be known only as Running Free.

The Peachy Talbot Fan Club
by Carmel Lockyer

When Peachy first asked me for a date, I didn't laugh. I could have done; if it had been any other nerdy little guy with pebble glasses and albino eyebrows, I would have done. But I liked Peachy. Most people did. Correction. Most men like him. Women, as I was about to find out, just loved Peachy to death.

But as I say, that first time, I just smiled and said thank you, but … no thank you.

I mean, everybody knew I was getting over Rafe and the terrible way he'd dumped me. It was a bad, bad time for Peachy to even think about a date: if half the 49ers had appeared at the front desk with nothing on but their helmets, and serenaded me, I'd still have probably turned them down. Probably.

Peachy just smiled and carried on down the hall while I dragged out another file and started trying to work out if the consultant whose expense claim I was working through was stupid, insane or unable to stay on the right side of the law.

Within ten seconds Mariella Saunders had popped her head up over the cubicle wall and wagged her finger at me.

"You turned down a date with Peachy? You crazy?"

I stared up at her, still mainly preoccupied with what kind of engineer thought he could claim eight visits to Peppermint Elephant Strip Club as a legitimate business

43

expense.

"So?" I said.

"So, you crazy girl, you just chase that sweet man down the corridor and make that date firm!" With that her head disappeared again.

Well I didn't, of course. I mean … Peachy? How desperate did she think I was?

The next day I saw Connie from the Human Resources department wandering along the corridor with a big dreamy smile on her face and, I swear, candy pink varnish on her toes. I'd never seen her before without the really thick American Tan pantyhose she wore all year round.

Mariella came and sat with me in the cafeteria. "So?" she asked.

"So what?" I replied

"You didn't do it!" Her face fell like somebody'd called the lottery numbers and hers had come up the one week she hadn't bought a ticket. "You missed your date!"

I shrugged. She might be trying to cheer me up but I thought it was pretty cruel of her to pretend Peachy was any kind of a catch, even if I had proved myself to be a complete moron with Rafe. Then she started looking round the room, like she was trying to catch somebody's eye.

"I wonder who it was then … have you seen anybody looking really happy this morning?"

I remembered Connie and the toenails and told Mariella.

"Oh, what a shame it wasn't you!" She sounded really put out. Her attitude was making me as mad as spit on a griddle, and I told her so.

"Really, Kath, I'm disappointed in you." She turned away from me and started to stir her iced tea so fast it slopped all over the edge of the glass. "Have I ever given you bad advice before?"

I thought about it for a second. Apart from the time she said I looked good in that pair of red hipsters that actually made my butt resemble two beef tomatoes wrapped in cellophane, the time that she suggested I consult a tarot reader who gave me nightmares by telling me I was going to have a career in the air when I have a flying phobia, and the time she persuaded me that five tequila slammers were the perfect preparation for Karaoke at the staff Christmas party, I had to admit that she'd never really given me bad advice.

"I'm sorry, Mariella," I said. "Just put it down to the whole Rafe thing. But you can't really expect me to dance for joy because Peachy asked me on a date?"

She leaned towards me. "Kath, you might not dance for joy beforehand, but believe me, you'll be dancing afterwards. Look at Connie."

She wouldn't say any more. It really bugged me. And when I saw Connie later in the day she was running her fingers over the top of the photocopier in a suggestive fashion that I'd never imagined of her.

So yeah, when Peachy asked me for a date a few days later, I said yes.

We went out for dinner, to a place with a deck that overlooked the beach. It wasn't romantic exactly, and nor was Peachy. I did my best to look at him with new eyes as we ate, but he was still Peachy, a really nice guy, but a short guy, a scrawny guy, a guy with clean fingernails and a natural line of conversation, Peachy whom everybody liked to talk to, because he was polite and good tempered, but he was no heart-throb.

He asked me to come back to his apartment for coffee. That was the first big surprise, because he didn't seem the least bit nervous about the invitation, in fact his pale blue eyes were sparkling with total confidence that I'd say yes. And, remembering Mariella's cryptic hints, I did say yes.

The second big surprise was Peachy's home. It was clean and bare and very attractive. He had Indian blankets on the wall, and lots of books and plants, and the whole place felt just as neat and wholesome as Peachy himself.

But around his bed were gauzy curtains in warm shades and when he pulled back those curtains, I saw the biggest bed my eyes had ever set on.

Man, did he ever need it.

The third surprise was Peachy's first kiss. He placed his index finger under my chin and kissed me so damn thoroughly that without his finger there to remind me that I needed to stay standing up, I think I would have melted to the floor right there. I don't think any man every kissed me with such attention to detail. He was tender and penetrating and his lips were supple and his teeth nibbled on my bottom lip in a way that made me wetter than the Mississippi in a flood and his tongue insinuated its way into my mouth with a kind of certainty that suggested this man knew exactly when, and exactly how and exactly where to do all the things no other man had known.

About twenty minutes later I could have been examining just how clean Peachy's bedroom ceiling was, if I hadn't been yelling my head off in the throes of orgasm. About ten minutes after that, I could have been counting Peachy's C.D. collection as I hung halfway off his big bed, with my head nearly on the floor and my feet locked around his neck as I more or less sat on his lap. He lifted my hips with his hands and thrust himself into me so perfectly that I orgasmed again. Then we had a short break where I remembered how to breathe more slowly and Peachy stroked my hair, and then, maybe an hour and a half after I first set foot in Peachy's apartment, I had my third orgasm with my face pressed hard into his pillowcases and my ass in the air, while Peachy knelt behind me and finally, amazingly, we came together.

But that's not why Peachy Talbot has a fan club. It's what happens afterwards that makes Peachy into the phenomenon he is. And for me, it went like this.

"I'm so happy you're here," he said, fitting himself into a spoon shape behind me and tracking patterns on my

46

shoulder blades with his warm, soft fingers. "I've always thought you have the loveliest skin: it's like amber, as if it's lit from within. You know, on days when it's raining and you come into the office, when I see the raindrops on your face, it doesn't look like rain, it looks like honey, golden sweetness, on your skin."

Okay, it sounds a bit schmaltzy. But he went on, to talk about my burgundy Nubuck shoes and how they made my insteps look kissable, and my diamond and garnet earrings that I inherited from my grandmother and only wore on special occasions like office parties. I mean, the man had noticed! I'd never met a man before who even knew what a garnet was, let alone who could have noticed a pair of earrings worn probably twice in his view. And he talked about the scar on my ankle I got when I fell over in fifth grade, and the time I had my hair cut really short and he could see how it made mahogany coloured ringlets in the nape of my neck and so on. It was like all the times I'd ever wanted a man to notice something hadn't been wasted: Peachy had just been storing up all those moments to give back to me.

So I thought I ought to do something for him. Which meant making sure he was up to it, and so it was something of a surprise when I reached behind me to find he was more than ready, and, in fact, when I took a good look at my instrument of passion, I discovered that while the rest of Peachy might be pale and on the small side, his cock was a large and rosy shaft, throbbing slightly and absolutely ready for me. And so I climbed on top of Peachy and my last coherent thought was that it was a long time since I'd felt comfortable enough with a man to stop thinking about my imperfections and inadequacies and just get on with getting it on.

But it didn't quite work out how I'd planned. I had another chance to inspect the ceiling, but I was too busy coming to really notice it. Then somehow we'd rolled over and our legs were tangled together as Peachy grinned at me with his perfect white teeth and slammed into me with his perfect tackle until I came again. And finally there was a long slow, comfortable half hour or so where I seemed to drift in and out of sleep and every time I came round I could feel Peachy sliding into me and out of me as gently as the tide, until I came, I swear to whatever gods there are, in slow motion. It was great. It was wonderful. It was incredible beyond compare. And despite my good intentions, I had the strong feeling that Peachy had just done for me what I'd been planning to do for him.

Still, I thought to myself, as I fell asleep for real. There was always next time.

Peachy woke me at one in the morning with green tea and a huge, clean, warm towel in which he wrapped me before leading me to the bathroom, where he had run a bath with rose and geranium bath oils. He washed me. Oh boy, how inadequate it is to say he washed me! His small, warm fingers covered every inch of my body in the warm water until I couldn't stop myself begging him to bring me off again, which he did, under the water, his eyes fixed on mine and mine on his. Mind-blowing was how it was, right down to the rose-scented water lapping at the sides of the bath with every thrust of his fingers and the way my slippery wet legs rose higher and higher out of the bath until I thought I'd either gone to heaven or learnt to breathe underwater.

Then he dried me, dressed me, drove me home, walked me to my door, kissed me and asked if he could call me again. Call me? He could have tattooed his number across my chest in fluorescent ink!

I slept like a baby. It was the first night I hadn't woken up reaching for Rafe, and the next morning I dressed carefully, putting on the burgundy Nubucks and the diamond and garnet earrings. I felt like a million dollars.

Melissa smiled at me. She smiled at me over the top of my cubicle before I'd even sat down. She smiled a great big 'cat that got the cream and the smoked salmon too' smile and asked me a question.

"Why do you think he's called Peachy?" she asked.

I shrugged, but I couldn't stop my own smile, a great big 'cat that got the cream, the smoked salmon and the lobster tails' smile.

She winked at me. "How do you feel this morning? Do you feel, maybe … peachy?"

I started to giggle. So did she. Eventually she laughed so much she fell off her chair and hit her chin on the cubicle wall and I had to run round to her side and hold ice in a napkin to her face so it didn't swell up.

So that was my first date with Peachy Talbot. And that set the pattern for all the others. There were things to get used to, of course. Like the fact that you never got to see Peachy more than once every three weeks or so, as he had a lot of dates. Like knowing that half the women in the firm were also on Peachy's list. Like however good he was in bed, and he was good, Peachy wasn't the kind of man you could tell a smutty joke to. He wasn't a prude, don't get me wrong, but he didn't have a dirty mind. That was part of his charm, in a way – his generous nature and his decency meant that you didn't ever wonder if he was talking about you behind your back, or making comparisons. Peachy was just … peachy, and any woman who'd spent a night with him would have trusted him with her life. Well, more than her life. Imagine if you had influenza, and hives, and a spot on your nose, your roots were growing out and you hadn't waxed your legs for two weeks, your robe was ratty, the sink was full of dishes and your only houseplant had died. There's only one man I'd open the door to if I were in that state – Peachy Talbot.

And so we carried on for about a year. When Rafe reappeared, about four months after he'd dumped me and left a pile of debts for me to pay, he expected to sweep me into bed and sweep himself back into my bank account. But

I took one long look at him, and thought of all the things he'd never noticed and never done, and how one little man with a love of women had made me feel like a princess when Rafe had never made me feel like more than a sucker and I kicked him so hard in his underperforming equipment that he was still on the ground, rolled up and wheezing, when I opened the door several minutes later to throw out the old football trophies that he'd left behind when he rabbited.

Peachy was a sex machine that I shared with who knows how many other women, except I knew about Mariella, and Connie, and a couple of others in the firm who were friends. But we never talked about it. It was like he infected us with his own good manners and reticence. If you'd had a 'peachy' night, you just smiled at your friends and they knew ... damn, did they ever know!

Sometimes, when I looked round the cafeteria, I'd get to wondering. What about Mrs Hanrahan, the Managing Director's Personal Assistant, who wore dresses with lace collars and had a gold rinse to cover up her grey – could she be one of us? What about Libuela Creula, the cafeteria manager from Cuba who was reputed to be a Santiera practitioner? Did she get to visit Peachy's big wonderful bed? But it was just idle curiosity until the day that Mariella called a meeting in the Ladies Restroom.

I saw the notice when I went in to brush my hair before starting work. 'RELOCATION PROPOSAL' it read: 'There is a plan to relocate the seismological survey team to the Colorado office. Any woman who feels she may be affected by this proposal should come to a meeting in the Cafeteria after work this evening – which will remain open for this purpose.'

And then it hit me. Peachy was a seismologist.

That night there were eleven of us in the cafeteria. Libuela sat glowering at the floor – so at least one of my questions was answered. Mariella took the chair.

50

"We are all met here for one reason, but just to be sure we're all in the same boat, I'm going to ask you to write down two letters on the paper in front of you, fold it up and hand it up to the front. If the letters are the right ones, we'll proceed, if they're not, I'll ask that person to leave before we continue. The letters I'm looking for are the initials of a certain person who is the reason for our concern."

We all scribbled on our papers. Mariella opened them up and nodded briskly at each one until, "H.T.?" she queried.

We all looked around and our eyes were caught by Connie's scarlet face. "Hugo Talbot," she muttered.

Mariella nodded magisterially but I had to giggle: I'd never stopped to wonder what Peachy's real name was. Libuela transferred her glare from the floor to me and I stopped chuckling – I didn't want some Santiera curse imposed on me.

"I take it we're agreed that this can't be allowed to happen?" Mariella asked.

"If'n that boy goes to Colorado – I go too," Libuela stated. I had a strong mental picture of her sitting on his bed like an ebony goddess, and then I saw all of us, one after another, on his bed, naked, sprawled, laughing, full of excitement and loving the way he made us feel. I imagined each of us: hiding behind the curtains with pretend shyness, performing striptease acts, standing on his bed and glorying in our nakedness, lolling, laughing, prone, supine, begging, daring, screaming with pleasure, drowsing, rolling around … we couldn't let him go.

"So what do we do?" I demanded.

"Unofficial action," Connie replied. "We can't do anything formal because …"

Well, we all know why not – a dozen women insisting that their pocket-sized love god shouldn't be moved to the other end of the country was going to make national news – international news even. We'd be the laughing stock of the engineering community.

"We make it clear that if Peachy goes, this firm won't be worth working in," Mariella concurred.

Libuela smiled startlingly. "Oh yes," she said. "That we can do!"

When I went to the powder room the next day, the notice had been changed. Now it said 'The P.T. Fan club – remember: your actions can guarantee a happy ending.'

The food in the cafeteria became inedible. Human Resources failed to process any holiday requests. I sat on the expense claim forms until cash-starved engineers in hard hats and big boots began to turn up at the office; haranguing the receptionists and glaring at anybody with a briefcase as though such a person might be stealing out the expenses money from under their noses. The only person whose expenses went through, whose coffee was hot, whose holiday was agreed – was Peachy.

We met again, after a fortnight. The dissatisfaction in the firm was tangible. You could taste it in the lumpy macaroni, hear it in the bad-tempered growls of the staff, sense it in the prickly glances that senior managers shot at everybody they passed in the hall.

"We seem to be having an effect. But how do we translate it into the action we want?" Mariella asked.

"We could bring down a hex," Libuela said. There was a short silence and then we all spoke at once to hide our own disquiet.

It was during this babble that I looked up and saw Peachy in the doorway. We fell quiet. I felt myself begin to blush. Then he held up the notice from the Ladies' Room.

"Thank you all, I feel honoured," he said. I can't speak for anybody else, but I blushed worse than ever.

"We can't let you go," Mariella said.

Peachy took off his glasses and rubbed them on the hem of his shirt. "Well, I don't see how you can stop it," he said. "The firm has to relocate the department, it makes economic sense."

"Give us one more week," Mariella replied. She sounded more confident than I felt.

When the invoices didn't get paid, our stock started to slide a little, and there was a board meeting called to explore why the firm had become so inefficient all of a sudden. Although everybody was supposed to be at hard at work, the eleven of us naturally gravitated towards the cafeteria. Libuela served us black coffee with guava and cream cheese refugiados. After a short while Mariella wiped her mouth, sighed in satisfaction and said, "Ready to rumble?" We all nodded, although I don't think anybody had the faintest idea what she was talking about.

She pulled out a mobile and punched a number. Two minutes later Mrs Hanrahan appeared in the doorway. She was wearing a navy blue shirtwaist with a crocheted collar and she held a sheaf of papers in her hand. Her face was puzzled. "This had better be as important as you claimed, Mariella, because I am meant to be taking minutes at the board meeting."

Mariella smiled. "We can solve the problems the board is debating, Mrs H. The eleven women in this room can put the firm back on its feet in a week. There's just one thing …"

And that's how Peachy became Colorado Liaison. He spends three months of the year in Colorado, broken into six fortnightly sections. The Peachy Talbot Fan Club cleans his apartment and waters his plants while he's away, and when he's back, Peachy Talbot divides his nights between us as he always did.

As for the 49ers, if they appeared butt-naked in reception, I'd suggest they took lessons from Peachy. There's only room for one sex god in my life – and that's why I'm a fully paid up member of the Peachy Talbot Fan Club. And so is Mrs Hanrahan …

Paper Rose
by J.S. Black

South East London 1967

From his corner desk within the busy office, Detective Ray
Morecambe observed the two women from over the rim of
his steaming coffee cup with interest.

He'd always enjoyed being able to discreetly appreciate
Officer Jenny White's full shapely thighs that she struggled
to contain within the thin material of her above-the-knee
skirt, always such a tempting distraction from so much dull,
routine paperwork.

But there was something about her female companion
that troubled him.

He assumed the other woman had been attacked judging
from her scuffed appearance and yet hers was not the face
of the beaten and frightened, instead she appeared to be
quite calm as she spoke quietly with Officer White. The two
seemed almost intimate in their conversation, such was their
closeness.

There was something familiar about her beautiful yet
strong features but his brain failed to make the right
connections and it bothered him.

His attention was drawn to the woman's hands. She was
toying with what appeared to be a pink rose and it could
almost have been a moment of tenderness when she handed

the flower over to Jenny White, who considered the flower before placing it upon the table. Morecambe watched their lips moving as they spoke. Jenny leaned forwards, placing a hand upon the other woman's thigh when she seemed to be trying to reassure her in some way.

Not for the first time Morecambe found himself trying to work out the enigma that was Officer Jenny White. He could describe her as being hardworking, determined and reliable but she was also a quietly sexual woman, alluring and strangely animalistic in her nature. And yet there was depth to her, a certain *darkness* that had intensified since the tragic loss of what had been *her* husband and *his* friend. He supposed he would always have to be content with admiring her from afar, when he'd secretly hoped that the death of a mutual friend might actually bring them closer together …

Morecambe began glancing over his papers when Jenny got up from her seat and headed towards him. He felt his face flush a little and wondered if she'd been aware of his voyeurism.

"Ray, I need to have a quick word with you." Morecambe looked up from his papers and into Jenny White's serious yet pleasant face.

"Certainly, what's on your mind?" Morecambe indicated towards the chair on the other side of his desk. Jenny pulled the chair to the side of the desk so that she would be closer to him and he felt immediately intoxicated by the woman's scent, her closeness forcing him to battle against his urge to kiss her.

"Ray, I have reason to believe the woman sitting over there has been attacked by the one we've been after, you're familiar with his calling card …"

"The paper rose, yes, of course," Morecambe glanced over Jenny's shoulder. The woman had picked up the paper flower from the desk, its bright pink appearing so much more vivid against the whiteness of her thigh on which it rested. She looked down at the fake flower thoughtfully before running her hand through her hair, pushing a blonde lock from her eyes. She turned her head and suddenly Morecambe found her enchanting eyes holding his own. The young woman was beautiful.

"… scum deserve the gallows."

"Sorry?" Morecambe turned his attention back to Jenny although the other woman's face remained in his mind as he struggled to remember where he might have seen her before…

"The scum out there, who dirty the air by their very existence, they deserve nothing less than the gallows," Jenny said, anger hardening her otherwise soft features.

"Yes, quite," Morecambe found himself looking deeply into Jenny's dark brown eyes and knew he'd become lost in them should he look for too long. "I'd better speak to her," he struggled to pull himself together, "she must be able to give us a description …"

"Ray, listen, let me stay with her, I believe she'll open up to me, she really needs someone who understands right now."

"By that you mean another woman, right? Yes, I suppose I can understand that. But you know she could be the link we're after." Morecambe felt a warmth wash over him when Jenny smiled. "What's her name?" he asked.

"Moira McCann. She wants to go home, Ray, she's upset, she needs to be in surroundings in which she feels comfortable …"

"Jenny, you know you're not supposed …"

"Trust me, Ray, I have a feeling about this," Jenny persisted. She placed a hand on his arm and Ray sighed in defeat.

"Okay, I suppose you're right, do what you need to do," he told her as he looked towards the woman, instinctively his mind began searching through its huge database once again, searching for something that he just couldn't find.

When Detective Ray Morecambe returned with fresh coffee the two women were gone. Upon Jenny's desk lay a single paper rose looking strangely out of place in the confines of the otherwise dull office.

Officer Jenny White followed Moira McCann up the flight of stairs leading to the apartments. Jenny admired the other woman's legs and longed to touch them once again. She imagined what it might be like to kiss their smoothness, to rest the softness of her cheek against those soft thighs.

She breathed in more deeply, eager to locate more of Moira's unusual yet exotic scent and tried to comprehend what it was about this woman that excited her so much…

Morecambe placed the rose on top of the filing cabinet before pulling open a drawer and finger-danced over the folders, stopping only when he reached the area he sought. He knew he was following nothing more than a hunch but more often than not he'd been right. Although for Jenny's sake he hoped that this time his hunch would be proven wrong.

Moira McCann unlocked the door to her apartment. She pushed the door open before stepping back and motioned for Jenny to enter.

Morecambe stared in disbelief at the open file before him. There could be no mistaking the small photo accompanying the file. It was definitely her. It disturbed him to think that such an attractive woman should have a record, spanning from prostitution to the more disturbing violent sexual conduct, towards both sexes, to her name.

And if that wasn't enough, her name, according to the file, wasn't Moira but *Rose* McCann, Rose McCann who took pleasure in mutilating pimps, drug dealers and just about anyone else whom she considered unworthy of the skin they're in.

Rose, it had seemed, had also gathered the nickname of "Paper Rose", so called due to her calling card that was a ...

Morecambe looked up at the rose upon the filing cabinet.

Slamming the drawer shut and spilling his coffee, Morecambe headed for the door at speed.

"I've always liked these apartments," Jenny said cheerfully as she turned to smile politely at Rose who had quietly shut the door behind her. Jenny's smile died upon her face when she saw the coil of rope that the woman held. In her other hand she held a gun. It was directed at Jenny.

And there was no politeness in Rose's smile at all.

Bringing his car to a screeching halt before the building, Detective Morecambe only hoped that the address he'd found in Rose McCann's file was valid. He fumbled with the door of the Jaguar in his haste to be inside the block and to locate apartment 4b, not wanting to admit to himself what he might do should he discover Jenny in any way harmed. The detective felt a little disgusted with himself when the mere thought of the woman caused a stirring in his loins, how could he be thinking of her sexually when she could be in such terrible danger?

He bounded up the stairs two at a time, his mind a turmoil of racing thoughts until the door marked '4b' bought him to a halt. He took a deep breath before delivering a firm rap upon the door.

No answer.

From somewhere inside the detective heard what sounded like a muffled plea. Reaching into one of his seemingly bottomless pockets Morecambe fished out his special key and with an expert turn the lock clicked open.

Morecambe decided to go on as he'd begun and unapologetically rushed into the room.

The sight that greeted him stopped him dead in his

tracks…

In the centre of the apartment was situated a high heavy oak
table. Securely tied to this table was Officer Jenny White.

Jenny's skirt had been pulled up over her hips, and her
bottom, raised due to the cushions placed under her, was
naked but for the small turquoise cotton panties doing little
to conceal the smooth white globes of her plentiful
buttocks. It was with effort that the detective wrenched his
gaze from the small moist patch upon the gusset. There was
a long ladder in her right stocking running down the length
of the back of her thigh and she had lost one of her shoes.
Jenny, he noticed, had also been gagged and blindfolded.

Also gathered upon the table were a small collection of
sex toys to which Morecambe had little doubt had been put
to some use upon Officer Jenny White.

"Oh … my … Lord …" the words tumbled from
Morecambe's lips before he could think to stop them.

When Jenny tried to speak from behind the gag her
words were incomprehensible to Morecambe who was
secretly pleased that she was unable to see his excitement,
something that would've proved difficult to hide as he
walked towards her. He tried to speak in an effort to both
comfort her and to tell her that he was going to get her out
of here and yet he couldn't wrench his gaze from the sight
of her, a sight more pleasurable than anything he'd before
imagined.

"Welcome, Detective," Morecambe was startled by the
voice behind him, "so glad you could make it." He turned to
see Rose McCann who had been silently hiding behind the
door. She aimed the pistol directly at his chest and the
beginnings of a smile etched across her red-glossed lips.

"What the hell do you think your game is? You won't
get away with this!" Morecambe told her. A muffled sound
came from Jenny.

"Oh, Detective, I do so hate to sound corny but is that a

59

gun in your pocket?" Rose glanced down at the obvious bulge in Morecambe's pants. To his embarrassment Morecambe found that he was evidently more excited than before and felt his face redden when his old friend 'shame' raised its ugly head once more.

"At the sight of you," the detective sneered, "it's a wonder it hasn't vanished up my arse!"

"Oh, now you *know* you don't really mean that," Rose said not unpleasantly.

Morecambe gave her the once over as best he could with a gun pointing at him and knew that she was right, he didn't mean it. The woman was stunning. He noticed that most of the buttons on her blouse were unfastened.

"Enough of this talk, Detective," Rose raised the gun slightly to let him know that he was still very much under threat, "turn to face her, it's time we had a little action going on here."

"I don't know what you intend to do but don't I even get a drink first?"

"Just do the fuck as I say," Rose ordered.

Morecambe turned and was faced once again with Jenny's raised bottom and once again a wave of sheer lust washed over him. His cock ached pleasantly as though sensing the closeness of the woman he'd desired for so long.

"Come on, you know you want this, she's gorgeous, I'd screw her if I had a dick, who do you think got her so wet for you?" Rose nodded towards the implements upon the table, her own excitement evident in her voice.

"Is this the only way you can get off Rose, by watching other folk fuck?" Morecambe asked, realising that he was only trying to sound under pressure for Jenny's benefit.

"Not at all, Detective, I merely consider this to be art, art to be enjoyed," she moved her position so that Morecambe could see her once again and would be aware of the gun still trained upon him. "Now, slowly, unfasten your pants, drop it all to the floor, I want to see your cock."

"I don't believe this …"

"Just do it."

Morecambe released each brace-strap from his shoulders before releasing the button on his slacks. They fell about his feet in a heap. His erection protruded from under his jacket and he looked almost apologetically towards Rose who observed his manhood. Her tongue flicked lightly over her lips, wetting them.

"Now, take off your jacket, shirt and shoes, kick them all away from you," Rose ordered, a quiet deepness in her tone now. Morecambe did as he was told.

"Boy, do you two look sweet," Rose teased when he was naked behind Jenny.

"Jenny, I'm so sorry about all of this," Morecambe said, to which Jenny mumbled something that the detective took to be an "OK". He looked down at his cock, it pointed directly towards the dark patch on Jenny's gusset.

"Sorry my ass, you look anything but sorry from where I'm standing," Rose giggled, "now, be a gentleman and remove the good lady's panties for her, nice and slowly mind as I'm still inclined to shoot your cock off should you piss me off."

"How do you expect me to do anything with a gun pointing at me? You'll never get away with killing two police officers …"

"Just do as I tell you and no one will get hurt,' Rose told him, "Now come on, get to it."

The detective moved forwards obediently and hooking his fingers into the elastic of Jenny White's panties, pulled them slowly over the firm smoothness of her bottom and down over her thighs. He needed to stoop down in order to release the garment over Jenny's feet and found himself facing her glistening sex.

"Taste her, make her wetter,' Rose ordered, eagerness apparent in her voice now.

"Forgive me Jenny, I'll ..."

"Do it!" Rose hissed, raising the gun once more.

Detective Morecambe, on his knees, began to taste Officer Jenny White. He no longer cared that he was being watched, no longer cared for the danger he was in or even that a gun was directed towards him. He drank in the scent of this woman, relished her moisture upon his face as he began to taste her, running and flicking his tongue between her thighs, feeling the sweet bud of her clitoris under the steady pressure of his eager tongue.

A muffled groan from Jenny White served only to make him want to pleasure this woman more. He lapped Jenny's abundant moisture, never before had he felt so aroused, so overwhelmed by the force of his own swelling lust.

"That's the way, now that looks so damn good, Mr Detective sir," Rose said with a sigh, "You know what? I believe she's ready for you now, Detective, what with your tongue and my ground work she must be damn near gagging."

Morecambe observed the collection of sex toys and silently wished he'd been here to witness the event, the thought excited him further. If he were unobserved he'd have put one to his mouth ...

"Stand up, Detective," Rose ordered. He noticed that although she still had the pistol trained upon him, her left hand had disappeared under her short skirt. Her breathing too had deepened.

"Slowly, I want to see you slowly push your cock into her," Rose commanded. She gazed intently at the detective's cock as though willing it forwards towards its goal and her pace upon herself quickened slightly.

"Lady, it's somewhat off-putting trying to do this with a pistol trained upon me," Morecambe protested.

"I'm sure you'll manage somehow, now do as you're told," Rose commanded impatiently.

"I'm so sorry, Jenny, but I have no choice, I will do my

utmost to be gentle with you," Morecambe told the gagged and blindfolded Jenny whose response was an eager squeal of consent, she too, it seemed, was reluctant to annoy her demanding kidnapper. The detective fought hard to contain his smile of pleasure when, with one hand resting upon the female officer's bottom he used his other to guide himself forwards into her and was deliciously enveloped by Jenny's silky warmth.

"Boy, that must feel so damn good, I do so envy you. Explore her with your hands too, damn you, come on, get into it, I want to see you use her!" Rose ordered excitedly, her fingers working hurriedly now between her thighs, Morecambe could hear her wetness, wished he could have her too.

Morecambe moved slowly at first, tentatively, but soon his own desire compelled his thrusts to quicken and deepen, the act becoming taken over by an inner animal instinct and audible slaps sounded around the room. He was encouraged further by the pleasurable sounds from Jenny.

The detective felt distracted when Rose moved to a position behind him and uneasiness settled in again now that she wasn't in view.

Something cool and smooth moved slowly over his thighs and buttocks and Morecambe surmised that Rose was using the pistol upon him, the sensation was not, he found, altogether unpleasant despite the danger he knew himself to be in.

When a switch was flicked and the object being used upon him began to vibrate he felt the beginnings of a warm tingling sensation signalling the onset of orgasm and knew that he couldn't last much longer. The vibrating object moved over his heavy scrotum and towards where his cock joined with Jenny, the toy now pleasuring her too and she let out a deep groan from behind her gag.

Morecambe made a conscious effort to slow his thrusts in a bid to gain control, knowing that there would be nothing to gain from finishing this too early. But even as the detective was becoming lost in his own pleasure the thought crossed his mind that maybe he could tackle Rose now that she'd made the mistake of getting too close. But it seemed that the woman had read his thoughts.

"Don't even think about turning around, Detective, you'd better believe it when I tell you that I still have the gun pointed in your direction. Do you really want a secondary arsehole? Now screw her hard."

Jenny White let out a muffled scream when her orgasm powered through her and Morecambe could hold back no longer. From behind him he heard Rose let out a deep sigh, an expulsion of her own lust, its breath warm upon his thrusting buttocks. He managed to pull his cock from Jenny's opening and was almost alarmed by the intensity of his own powerful orgasm when stream after stream of hot semen began to coat the pale globes of Jenny White's bottom.

"You really don't have to keep pointing that thing at me, lady," Morecambe nodded towards the pistol in Rose McCann's hand. The detective had been allowed to pull up his shorts and stood now in the middle of the room next to the large table that had held Jenny White.

Jenny was sitting next to Rose on the sofa. Her hands were tied and she still had the gag in her mouth and the blindfold around her eyes. Morecambe felt glad that he'd been allowed to cover himself up, not wanting Rose to see the excitement building him in once more.

"I'll tell you what, Detective, why don't I ask a member of your own team what I should do?" Rose kept the gun trained upon Morecambe while pulling both the gag and the blindfold from Jenny.

"Hell, that was damn good!" Jenny White said and Morecambe was surprised to see the smile spread upon her pretty face.

"Huh?" was all he could manage to blurt out.

Rose, with the beginnings of a smile upon her lips, pulled out a cigarette and placed it between her lips, her eyes never leaving the detectives. When she raised the pistol the detective feared that she would aim it towards Jenny. His body tensed, ready to spring forward.

Rose held the barrel of the gun to her cigarette. She pulled the trigger and a small flame popped from the end of the barrel. Inserting her cigarette into the flame, she lit it.

"You just can't beat a smoke after a good fuck, wouldn't you agree, Detective?" Rose asked.

"Bad for your health," the detective said through clenched teeth, "Just what the hell is going on here?" Morecambe demanded, realising for the first time the closeness of the two women upon the sofa.

"Come on now, Ray, you have to admit that was good, don't tell me you didn't enjoy any of what just happened here?" Jenny asked. She lit the cigarette between her own lips from the offered flame.

"Let's just say that it was an experience." Morecambe looked to each of the women in turn. They both smiled gleefully which only added to his confusion. "Jenny, have you any idea who this woman is? She's dangerous," Morecambe implored.

"Don't believe the hype, she's a pussycat," Jenny answered. She gave the other woman's thigh a gentle squeeze and planted a lingering kiss upon her cheek.

"I've seen her file, damn it! She's a killer!"

Both women laughed. It was Officer White who spoke, "She's no killer, Ray, and she's certainly not this 'Paper Rose' that you've been after. We set you up, come on, admit it, you enjoyed it, you've wanted me for ages, you think I didn't know?"

For a moment Morecambe was silent. He observed the two half-naked women on the sofa before him and a smile formed upon his lips. Jenny moved over and patted the space between herself and Moira, inviting him to join them and by the time he'd reached them his smile had become a laugh silenced only by the women's hands upon him.

Officer Jenny White, alone now in her own apartment, reflected on what had proved to be a remarkable day. Pulling open an old drawer in her bedroom she dropped in the paper rose where it lay to rest with the many others. She looked down momentarily at the many fake flowers, her calling cards, and considered going out into the night before deciding against it. She felt tired and her bed called, so some lucky scumbag out there would be allowed to live if only for another night.

Today had been fun but tomorrow she must continue with her work, her life's work. Tomorrow night she would again attempt to clear the streets of its human filth, the kind of filth that had taken the life of her beloved husband.

Fantasy Assignment
by Lucy Felthouse

I couldn't believe my luck when I heard what my next editorial assignment was. In fact I discreetly pinched myself to make sure I wasn't dreaming.

My editor wanted me to write an article on Single Living Accommodation in the Army. The ARMY. "Big deal" I hear you thinking. Perhaps I'd better explain. I have a real thing about men in uniform, I always have had. Stick me in front of a hot guy in uniform and I'm putty in His hands. So you see I was rather excited at the prospect of being around all these sexy men. And even better, I was going to be paid for it. Talk about perks of the job!

The article was planned into an upcoming edition of the glossy women's magazine I work for. The 'careers special' was designed to give the readers an insight into different industries and jobs within them.

I only had a few days to prepare for my assignment, so I did my homework and made lots of notes. I always like to be well prepared, to avoid the chance of messing something up and getting a bollocking from the editor.

Soon enough, the day arrived and I dragged myself out of bed at 6am, a chore in itself as I'm not a morning person, got my things together and got a taxi to the train station. I had strict instructions on where I had to change trains, where I should go and who I should look for when arriving at my destination. Corporal Matt Stokes would be there waiting for me. Given he'd be wearing uniform, I wasn't too worried about recognising him.

When I boarded the first train and got settled into my seat, I grabbed my bag and pulled out a magazine. After reading the same page three times and realising I still had no idea what it was about, I gave up. I allowed my mind to wander. Would Corporal Stokes be attractive? Would he be tall and slim; small and well-built? Aloof, cheeky; who knew? All I knew for sure was that there was a good chance I'd think he was sexy simply because of what he was wearing. In my opinion, the uniform screams masculinity and sex. It hides what is beneath, leaving that to your imagination, but gives the impression of the wearer being rough and ready – just how I like my men.

After a speedy change of trains, I relaxed and let my thoughts wander for some time, until I heard the announcement that my station was the next one. I got myself ready, checked I had all my stuff together and perched on the edge of my seat. I was also aware that my daydreams had left me feeling more than a little horny, and as a consequence, my underwear was damp. I smiled to myself. I hadn't even set eyes on a squaddie yet and my mind was in the gutter. Heaven knows what I'd be like when I was surrounded by hard male bodies, and the smell of sweat and spunk.

Perhaps I would become immune to the charm of the uniform after seeing it constantly for a couple of days? Only time would tell. Five minutes to be precise; which was the time it took for the train to pull in at the platform and for me to get off and look around for my lift. As I'd expected, he wasn't difficult to spot. As soon as I laid eyes on the six foot plus frame of Corporal Stokes, I knew I would never get bored of that uniform as long as I lived. Especially on him.

Towering over most of the people milling around, he

stood against the wall, out of the way of the crowds. From where I stood I could see he had dark hair and eyes, and that was about it. I scraped a hand briefly through my hair and headed over to him.

He caught my eye as I approached.

"Corporal Stokes?"

"Yes ma'am."

Ma'am? What the fuck? Did he think I was royalty or something? Hell, who cared, it was damn kinky and this man could call me anything he wanted, whenever he felt like it. He was the most divine creature I'd ever laid eyes on. Your classic tall, dark and handsome sex god.

"I'm Charlene Collins. Good to meet you."

I stuck out my hand and he shook it, and then offered to take my bags. I let him. After all, he had the muscle for it, and I thought it was a damn good excuse to check out his arse as he bent to pick them up. It was definitely worth it. His combat trousers went taut and I had a good look at what I suspected was a nice firm backside. I quickly averted my eyes as he stood, then followed his lead as we left the station.

Parked outside was a dark green 4x4. What was I expecting, a limo? Trouble is, I had no idea how I was going to get in the damn thing, given I was wearing a tight pencil skirt with slits up the side and stiletto heels. Bollocks.

Corporal Stokes strode over to the vehicle, unlocked it and put my bags in the back. He was just about to open his door and hop in when he noticed me dithering on the passenger side. A slight frown on his face, he walked around to me. Then he appeared to really notice me for the first time. His eyes travelled from my beautiful but completely impractical shoes, to my tight knee-length skirt, and finally to my trendy white blouse, buttoned to reveal just a hint of cleavage. I saw the comprehension dawn on his face, followed by that slight frown again. In an instant, it was gone.

"Ma'am," he said, his eyes glinting with amusement, "let me help you. I'm going to have to lift you onto the seat. Watch your head."

He proceeded to steer me so I was facing him, my back to the truck. Then his hands were on my hips and lifting me as though I was weightless until my backside was resting on the seat. I could then easily swivel myself around to sit properly without displaying my underwear to the world. But I didn't. I remained frozen in place for a couple of seconds, Corporal Stokes' hands still on my waist until I steadied myself. Well, I was certainly in no rush for him to let go. Our eyes met. I felt a trickle of moisture between my thighs, and looked down, sure it was obvious to the world. But it broke the spell. Once our eye contact was severed, Corporal Stokes cleared his throat loudly as he removed his hands from my waist then stepped back and prepared to close the door of the truck when I was ready.

I hastily shuffled round so I was facing the right way and grasped the seatbelt with slightly trembling fingers, which didn't want to do their job. I managed to wrench it across my body and fumble around trying to clip it into place as Matt got into the driver's side of the 4x4. He hopped in effortlessly, fired the engine and put on his own safety belt. He glanced across at me to make sure I was secure, then wrenched the vehicle into gear before pulling out of the car parking space and heading for the exit.

As the countryside sailed past, I took advantage of the fact Matt was concentrating on driving and studied him as subtly as possible. I glanced at his profile. He really was what many women would consider a good catch. As I said, he was tall with dark hair and eyes. He also had a very sensual mouth with full lips which I could imagine doing all kinds of unspeakable things to me …

Ahem, anyway. As it was a warm day, he'd rolled the sleeves up on his shirt to reveal lovely muscular arms. I briefly wondered if his thighs would follow suit, then thought it probably wasn't a good idea to allow myself to think about what was under those combats. It could get me into all kinds of trouble.

In an attempt to distract myself, I made idle conversation with Matt. I found out his age (same as me, 25), how long he'd been in the Army, whether he'd been deployed before, and so on. He turned to glance at me occasionally as he answered my questions. Which I had lots of, according to him.

"I'm a journalist; it's my job to ask questions."

"But you're not writing an article about me!"

"No, but I'm just taking an interest in the nice young man that's kindly picked me up, is that a crime? I'm still human you know."

He had the good grace to look embarrassed.

"I'm sorry," he said, "it's just in my nature and my job description to be suspicious of everyone. I didn't mean anything by it."

"It's OK. Taking abuse is another part of my job role."

He grimaced. "I said I'm sorry. Look, we're nearly here."

I wasn't sure what we were supposed to be looking at, exactly. We were motoring through a quaint little village, which didn't look at all military. I didn't know what to expect, but my pervy frame of mind was hoping for dozens of men in uniform walking the streets. Damn my libido-driven imagination.

A few moments later we turned left up a long road which had a kind of gatehouse at the other end. We trundled up to the gates and were waved through after the guard had a cursory glance inside the truck, and nodded at me.

Matt manoeuvred the truck through the grounds and the groups of uniformed men (finally!). There were women too, of course, but I wasn't interested in them. Though I could certainly see the logic behind their career choice. He headed for some garages and pulled the vehicle inside, then killed the engine. Great, I thought, now I've got to attempt to get out of this damn thing. Preferably without flashing my pants.

I needn't have worried, though. Matt came to the rescue by jumping out of his seat and coming round to my side. He flung open the door and stood looking at me, an amused expression on his face. I flashed him a grin and swung my legs around to the side of the seat and made to slide down out of the seat, using Matt as a kind of fireman's pole. What happened next was somewhat of a blur. The most erotic damn blur of my life.

As I slid down with Matt helping me as gentlemanly as he could in the circumstances, I became very aware that I was rubbing my body against his. Now I wasn't too concerned by that fact, because I couldn't think of anything else I wanted more. Except to do the very same thing, naked. But I had no idea of how he felt about me, if he even found me attractive. A couple of seconds later, I knew the answer. My feet touched the floor, but I was in no hurry to move. Pressed tightly to Matt, I could feel his erection straining against the confines of his combats. His hands were still on my waist and as our eyes met, I felt his fingers tighten against my flesh, which sent a lightning bolt of arousal to my groin.

He wanted me as much as I wanted him, that much was obvious. But I also knew that he wouldn't do anything about it. He was at work; his job was on the line. Hell, so was mine. I could tell he was struggling with his conscience, so after shouting a firm internal "fuck off" at mine, I decided to bite the bullet. You only live once, after all.

I kissed him. No mean feat I tell you. Me being tiny, him towering over me and all. I just slipped my hands up to his neck and stretched up, pulling him down to meet me halfway. The moment our lips touched was electric. The combination of the situation, the risk, his attire and my overactive libido had my pussy oozing almost immediately.

Stunned at first, Matt barely moved, he just let me kiss him. But seconds later, it was as if a switch had been flipped. The little devil on his shoulder clearly won. Lucky me. He began kissing me back with gusto, one hand travelling north from my waist and tangling into my hair, pulling me closer and deepening the kiss.

Our tongues danced together, our hands caressed one another, and our groins – well, they did what groins do when they're sexually aroused. My tight skirt meant I couldn't press myself against his hardness as much as I'd have liked, but still. I knew a way I could fix that. As I pulled away to glance behind me at the still open door of the truck, strong hands lifted me back onto the seat I'd just vacated. They then proceeded to push at my skirt, bunching it up to get at what was underneath.

He lifted my ankles, placing my legs either side of his head and buried his face between my thighs. He nuzzled at my flesh, placing delicate kisses, then sharp little nips all over my skin. All the while he crept closer to the place that wanted him the most. I knew my panties would be drenched, and felt mildly embarrassed. What if he thought I was some kind of sex-mad hussy? Sex-starved more like.

I soon stopped worrying. He breathed in deeply and made an appreciative sound deep in his throat at the scent of my sex, which only served to arouse me more. I wanted him to touch me there, in my most secret place. Seconds later, he did. He pushed his nose and mouth to my vulva and breathed out deeply. His hot breath filtering through my pants to my pussy felt sublime, but I still wanted more. I pushed my hips towards him, hinting at what he should do.

Of course, he already knew what to do, he was just teasing me. Slender fingers of one hand crept up to join his face between my legs, and pulled my sticky knickers aside. I gasped at the contact, and then again as his tongue finally caressed my tortured pussy. He set to work licking up all the juices that had been secreted from my body, but as he did, my cunt continued to produce them. I realised he could be down there some time. Ah well, I thought, that's no hardship. He was damn good at what he was doing, too, gently nipping at my outer labia, and sucking them gently into his mouth, one at a time, then letting go and letting his tongue dance around. He flicked briefly at my clit, then teasingly went lower, to the entrance of my pussy, and teased me there.

As he gave me expert head, I felt my internal muscles tighten involuntarily. Then that familiar tingling feeling which told me an orgasm was on its way. To ensure Matt didn't stop pleasuring me at a crucial moment, I crossed my ankles behind his head and pulled him more firmly to me. He seemed to relish in this mild act of domination, and suckled at my clit almost savagely. And that was it, all it took to trigger my climax. I thrust my hands into his hair as I moaned my pleasure aloud, unwilling to let him go.

But Matt had other ideas. Grinning wildly at the result of his efforts, he leaned up to kiss me, his lips now sticky with my juices. I kissed him back, deeply, still high on passion. I could feel his erection through his trousers now, mere layers of fabric between his cock and my aching cunt.

"Fuck me, now." The words were out of my mouth before I knew it. Well, I couldn't take them back now. Matt didn't exactly resist, either. He unbuckled his belt, and undid his fly. Underneath he wore white boxers. My absolute favourite. His trousers dropped to his ankles as he stood on the step of the truck. He stroked his cock through his boxers and I longed to feel it inside me. But first …

I rooted around for my handbag and grabbed it, my fingers deftly opening it and diving into the inside pocket to retrieve an emergency condom. I always kept a couple in there, just in case. You just never know, do you? Horniness made my movements quick and precise. Within seconds the wrapper was open and the protection ready in my hand. I beckoned to Matt and he leaned over me once more. I opened the buttons on the front of his boxers and pulled out his prick.

And I was so very glad I did. It protruded proudly from his body, a lovely long and thick cock, nestling in nicely groomed pubic hair. I stroked it a couple of times and grinned as I saw the pre-come seeping from the tip. It was so thick my hand barely fit around it, and I couldn't wait to have it buried deep inside me. I rolled the condom on firmly, then lay back and grabbed Matt's collar.

I yanked him down on top of me, his mouth met mine again and his lovely dick nestled against my wetness, my panties still shoved to one side. I pushed my hips towards his, hurrying him along. I wanted him, now. His resolve didn't last long. After sliding his length up and down my vulva a couple of times, he suddenly plunged inside. I was so wet that he sunk right in with no resistance at all. We moaned simultaneously at the sensation, I of being filled, he of being surrounded by wet warmth. Then he began to move inside me, slowly at first, then building up speed.

He alternated thrusts; some slow and deep; others fast but shallow. I looked into his eyes and knew he was teasing me once more. He somehow knew how I wanted it, but was deliberately holding back. I grabbed his gorgeous firm arse cheeks and pulled him roughly to me and thrust towards him at the same time. I needed it hard, fast, rough. I wanted to come again, spasming and squirting around his cock.

Now he couldn't resist. He began to piston into me like some kind of machine. Hard, fast, deep strokes that had me screaming in delight, or would have done had he not clamped a hand over my mouth. I gripped his arse like I would never let go, greedily pulling him into me.

I felt my second orgasm approaching and wrenched my face away from his hand.

"Come for me baby. I want to feel your cock pumping

its load into me as I come. Fuck me as hard and fast as you can go."

He didn't need telling twice. He certainly tested the suspension on the truck! I thought my pussy was on fire, the friction was so deliciously hot. I felt my pussy tighten once more, the telltale sign of my orgasm, then Matt slowed his pace …

"I'm coming baby – now."

The feel of his muscles contracting inside me gave me that final push. My own orgasm ripped through my body, more powerful than the last, making spots dance behind my eyelids and my back arch, pushing his cock yet deeper into me. We rode out our simultaneous climaxes, limbs entangled and breaths coming fast and shallow. He dropped down on to me, exhausted, his lips seeking mine for a tender kiss. I felt his heart beating madly against my chest, even through our clothes.

Conscious of where we were, we couldn't afford too much recuperation time so we kissed one final time and reluctantly began to rearrange ourselves.

Once decent, Matt held his hand out to help me out of the truck.

"Think you can keep your hands off me this time?"

"Looks like I'll have to."

A cough behind Matt drew his attention to a stern-looking older man approaching us. He looked as though he was in a senior position, and therefore Matt's boss.

"Charlene Collins?" The man questioned. I nodded and held out my hand.

"General Leadbetter, ma'am. I trust Corporal Stokes has been looking after you?"

"Oh yes, General. He's attended to my every need."

The Painter's Palate
by Joe Manx

My neck was getting really stiff. I don't know why I continued with this, the pay was pretty crap.

'Okay, let's take a break.'

I rotated my neck to ease the stiffness and moved off the couch.

'Are you OK, Julia, you look a bit uncomfortable?'

I began to answer but a student called out to the teacher. 'Fiona, could you just look at this?'

'I'll be right with you. Sorry, Julia, help yourself to tea, I'll be back in a moment.'

I moved towards the tea urn, massaging my neck, feeling the muscles gradually release some tension and begin to relax a little. Actually, the pay was crap but I enjoyed the work. How else would I get the opportunity to flaunt my naked body? I'd always enjoyed being a bit of an exhibitionist, this took it that step further and being an artist's model for the local college evening classes made it all very respectable. I knew, from my fixed vantage point, that not all of the students were there for the art. There were a few letches which added to the enjoyment. They could look but not touch. Delicious.

'Can I pour you a cup?'

I turned my head and saw a bright-looking young man holding a cup in front of his face and smiling. He looked innocent.

'Yes, please.'

'Sugar?'

'No thanks. I've not seen you before – are you new?'

'Yes, it's my second week. I must say you're an excellent model, what do you normally do for a job?'

'I'm training to be an accountant.'

He looked surprised.

'Thank you,' I said as he handed me the tea. 'What about you, what's your line of work?'

'Oh, I'm a bone fide artist.' He smiled, self consciously. 'Not a very successful one, but it's early days.'

I thanked him for the tea and moved back to the couch. During the second half of the session I had the opportunity to examine him a little more closely. Sweet, pleasant, naive. I liked him.

For the next few weeks, the young man, George was his name, attended the venue and we got to know each other a little better. If no one else had grabbed my attention he would sidle up to me with a cup of tea and talk.

After one session, about a month after our first meeting, I found George hanging around for me outside.

'Sorry to bother you, Julia, I hope you don't think I'm being creepy, but I wondered if you could do me a favour?'

I'd begun walking towards my car. He fell in beside me. I didn't find him creepy or threatening. I didn't think he was capable.

'What sort of favour?'

'Well, you know I'm an artist and a struggling one at that. Coming to evening classes is a cheap way of getting some practice in traditional methods. The work I'm currently developing uses more modern methods and techniques. At the moment, I desperately need models. I was wondering, could I use you and pay you later when I sell some work? I know it's a bit cheeky, but I'm sure I'll

sell some work soon … I'll quite understand if you say no.'
He looked at me imploringly, hopefully.

'Okay,' I said. I didn't particularly need the money and it sounded as though it might be fun. I felt a little excited at the prospect of teasing this young innocent. 'On one condition,' I said, 'make sure there's plenty of tea and biscuits.' I gave him my telephone number and left him beaming.

I got the call several days later and we arranged to meet the following week. George lived in rather a nice flat in a decent part of town. 'Somehow I expected the place to be a lot seedier,' I said , as I stepped through the front door, 'you know, struggling artist and all that.'

'I'm fortunate,' said George, 'my parents have helped me out, they bought this place as an investment and, at the moment, let me stay rent free.'

He showed me through to the main room which should probably have been a lounge. The room was almost empty of furniture save for a large sofa, several chairs and an old rug. The walls were covered with paintings and photographs. An easel stood in the middle of the room. There were smears of different coloured paints on the exposed floorboards. I took a closer look at some of the paintings and photographs. They were very good.

'This is the style I'm interested in at the moment,' said George, leading me to the wall at the far end of the room. There were a series of photographs of painted faces.

'Here,' said George, pointing to one, 'look at the way the colours highlight the different features of the face, the way it adds mood and atmosphere.'

He showed me an enlarged photograph of a redhead. He'd painted her face blue and the effect was striking. She looked more intense, richer, sexier, her red hair more vibrant. The picture was full of energy.

'What do you think?'

'It's lovely, so rich and lively, the colour draws your eyes to every part of the face. Look at the ears, I probably wouldn't have noticed those in an ordinary picture but they look so interesting. The photography heightens the effect.'

'Julia, I want to paint other parts of the body, including the more intimate parts, that's why I've had difficulty getting models. Like those faces, paint will highlight other features in an interesting way. I want to experiment not just with different colours but different textures. Imagine, say, the beauty of a breast. Now imagine it painted bright blue with yellow nipples or orange stripes, or partly exposed by flaking, cracked paint. Wouldn't that be interesting? Imagine your bottom all red or green. Imagine having painted stockings and suspenders? Think of all the different effects you could get, sexy, comical, confusing.

I'll understand if you refuse. It's quite a step being painted in the nude, but literally being painted is much more intimate and I would think, much more daunting. I'd quite understand if you weren't keen on the idea

I was a little surprised by this development. I thought George would be the one to be a little nervous but there was an intensity about him, a focus. I liked it. Here, talking about his work, his character had come alive. His shyness, his apologetic, physical stance, had disappeared. I examined the pictures again, they really were very good. I liked the idea. George's enthusiasm was attractive. I laughed at the images in my mind.

'Okay,' I said, 'sold.'

I left George beaming again, having agreed to start in a week's time.

I duly turned up the following Tuesday evening. George answered the door wearing loose, track-suit bottoms and a paint spattered sweatshirt. He took my coat and led me through to the sitting room where he'd thrown a pile of cushions on the floor. By the cushions were large tubes of paint, paintbrushes, some jars, filled with water, and some cameras.

'There,' he said, 'I thought cushions would probably be the most comfortable. Now, I think it's best if you just take your top off first.'

I removed my top and sat on the cushions.

'We'll start with your breasts.'

I leant back on my hands so that my tits stood out.

'Wow, that's great,' said George, trying to put me at ease. He needn't have bothered, I'd posed a hundred times before. I was unconcerned and the exhibitionist in me was eager to perform. George squeezed some paint onto a palette.

'I use poster paints for this,' he said, 'they're nice and thick with a smooth texture. This is made of sable,' he continued, as he dipped and rolled the brush in the paint. 'Ready?'

I found his seriousness quite amusing and smiled at him. The brush touched my breast and I felt a tingle of excitement. George began to paint my breast slowly and purposefully. Each stroke felt like a soft, smooth tongue. He paid particular attention to my nipple, moving the brush up and down and in circular motions, causing it to harden in response.

'That feels nice,' I volunteered.

'Good,' said George, whose concentration was fixed on my breast. I found his detachment rather alluring. He put down the brush, reached across for a camera and began to photograph my breast. After a minute or so he put the camera down and began to paint my other breast. My reactions were similar. My breasts were shiny blue and looked rich and smooth. He took more photographs.

'Now then, I just want to get another effect.' He went off and came back with a hairdryer which he plugged in and turned on. He directed the nozzle on to my tits and I felt my nipples again hardening as the warm air flowed over them, drying the paint and tightening the skin.

'That's great,' he said, when the paint had completely dried. He took more photos. 'Now, would you mind just pinching or massaging your nipples so that the paint around them flakes off? Just gently, if you don't mind.'

I was enjoying myself. I felt very comfortable with George and rather aroused.

'Like this?' I said, tweaking my nipples.

'Not too much, I just want a cracked, flaking appearance, as though your nipples are budding through, ready to bloom.'

'You show me,' I said, 'I don't want to spoil the effect.'

George took hold of my nipples, between his thumbs and forefingers and gently pulled and massaged them. Fuck, he was good. My breathing began to get heavier and just as I was about to moan out loud the bastard stopped.

'That's great,' he said, enthusiastically, and took some more photos.

'Okay, let's move down to your bottom and fanny.'

The casual way he said this made me laugh

'You still OK with this?' he said.

'Yeah , I'm fine, it's actually rather fun.'

'Right, let's do the rest of the body. Slip off the rest of your clothes.'

I did as I was told. I felt rather excited. George began to paint my body with a large decorator's brush. It was like having a gentle, sensuous massage. The long, soft strokes sent me into a kind of drowsy trance. My whole body relaxed. I closed my eyes to concentrate on the luxurious feelings. George painted my neck and ears, my shoulders, back and belly. He painted my toes and feet. Every so often, he would stop and take pictures, asking me to pose in different ways. I didn't want him to stop. 'Okay,' he said, 'now for your bottom. You OK?

I smiled at him . 'How do you want me?'

'Turn over and raise your bottom in the air.'

I wondered whether he would find my pouting bottom of artistic interest or whether it would arouse a more sexual response. I rested my head on a cushion, raised my bottom and parted my legs slightly. 'This OK?' I said. I heard a sharp intake of breath.

'Julia, you have a fantastic bottom, it's going to look superb painted. Are you sure you're going to be OK with my prying brush?'

'Actually, I feel very safe with you and I love the sensation of the brush on my skin, carry on.'

He began to paint my bottom. Again, the long sensuous strokes as he covered my cheeks in paint. I liked the idea of him looking at my bum. There was a pause in his strokes then I jolted as I felt the tip of the sable brush delicately touch the very entrance of my arse. I was a little shocked by the intimacy, but it felt divine.

'You OK?' said George.

'Yes, it feels wonderful, carry on.' I moved my arse a little higher, eased my legs a little further apart. George settled down and began to paint the puckered kiss. Not sweeping, long strokes, but delicate, short strokes. It felt as though he were painting each little ridge and groove, pinpointing tiny nerve endings with the soft, sable tip, causing glorious, intense, tingles of pleasure. I couldn't help but moan a little.

'Sorry,' I said, 'but that feels wonderful.'

'You go ahead,' said George, 'it would be a shame not to enjoy the experience, I am.' I heard him stand up and take more photographs. 'Julia, I can't thank you enough, you wait until you see the photos. Right, pussy next,' he said. 'I'm going to paint it yellow, if that's OK.'

'I don't think being coy at this stage would be very convincing,' I laughed. I remained, expectantly, on all fours. A few seconds later and I felt the soft brush strokes gently cover the lips of my pussy. Again, soft strokes of pleasure. Heavenly! George spent some time painting this area during which I moaned freely. After a while he told me to turn over. I felt marvellously relaxed with him. I sat upright, leaned back on my hands and spread my legs. George knelt down between them, brush in hand, and began to paint the upper parts of my pussy with deft, pointed touches that sent rivulets of pleasure coursing through me. His face was inches from my pussy and I could feel his warm breath, soft and pampering. I lay back on the cushions and widened my legs, to fully enjoy the sensations. George was delicately stroking my clitoris, now concentrating on my pleasure rather than any artistic effect. Inevitably, he brought me, shuddering and moaning, to orgasm. He pulled away, put down his brush, reached for his camera and stood up. He gave me a little while to recover.

'What's all this then?' I laughed, pointing to the obvious bulge in his trousers. He looked a little sheepish.

'Sorry, Julia, don't be alarmed, I wouldn't be human if I didn't have some sort of physical reaction. Besides,' he smiled, 'if this turns me on then it will turn others on and that's got to be a good thing.'

'Here,' I said, 'I've got an idea.' I leaned forward and yanked down his tracksuit bottoms. His cock sprang out, inches from my face. George was a little alarmed.

'I think your cock needs a lick ...' I said, in an exaggeratedly sexy voice, '... a lick of paint that is.'

He pulled back, not sure how to react.

'Come on,' I said, grabbing hold of his cock, 'let's call it interactive art.'

I made him lie on his back. I took a fresh, sable brush, dipped it in warm water, rolled it in blue paint and set about painting the shaft of his cock. It remained steadily erect. When I'd finished, I took another brush and rolled it in yellow paint, then delicately and slowly began to apply it to his purple glans. He let out groans of approval with each stroke. I began to giggle as the end of his cock turned a

84

bright yellow. I painted his balls pink, enjoying the look on his face as the slow, fine brushstrokes tickled and teased.

As I was creating my masterpiece an idea occurred to me. I began to masturbate him and at the same time I inserted the soft brush into his bottom, using slow brushstrokes and rotating the head from time to time. George was groaning with pleasure. I felt quite powerful. As I moved my hand more rapidly up and down his cock, the yellow paint on his glans began to mix with the blue paint of his shaft and part of his cock began to turn green. I began to laugh hysterically as he trembled beneath me and spurts of warm semen splashed onto my arm. I mixed his cum with the paint and stroked it back onto the end of his cock. The brushstrokes revitalised him and as he stood erect I took various pictures of his multi-coloured dick.

One thing led to another. We've become painting partners. Some of our first pieces sold quickly and initial interest helped us secure the services of other models. We had great fun producing a collage of multi-coloured cocks and fannies entitled 'Meat meets meatus'. It sold for a fair old sum. We've established a bit of a reputation.

Perhaps we'll end up as famous as Gilbert and George. Wouldn't that be nice?

The Examiner
by Roger Frank Selby

Reluctantly, the Examiner quit the purple sky and settled his craft deep into the clearing. The engines cut, and the slapping rotors slowly released their fury. A glance outside showed the expected monochrome carpet at the edge of the grass – mainly white-garbed women interspersed with the black of their remaining menfolk. The Disciple's winged-eye logo had them all on their knees.

After reporting safe arrival at village 921, he relaxed in the afterglow of flight, delaying for a moment the realities of life on planet Eden that would begin on opening the cockpit.

Too soon, the flash of a blue robe stirred him. He exited and strode towards the silver-haired man coming out to meet him, graciously reducing his vigorous stride to match the Village Master's dignified pace. 'Bless the Holy One!'

'May the Holy One be blessed. Welcome to Apostle Creek, Examiner! Your Journey was pleasant, I trust?'

'Yes, thank you Master; I always enjoy my flying.' They were technically of equal rank – it was safe to be this informal, but first: 'Lord Sevolian thanks you for your report and sincerely hopes that it is not exaggerated in any way.' Sevolian's exact words – standard intimidation a High Lord used on his Village Masters. That was how Eden worked, top-down terror, an unbroken chain from Disciple to peasant.

'I can assure you it is not!'

Some of the kneeling villagers stirred.

'Hush my brother, it is his Lordship that must be assured.'

'Of course, Examiner, I spoke hastily, but I am confident his Lordship will be delighted when you take her to him – as I am certain you will. Now, let's see … all men of military age are off-world on the Crusades, leaving mostly the women and girls. Aha! We are in luck – there she is! When I raise them you will see her. Over there, by the stocks.'

The Examiner glanced at the frames, manacles and chains. They appeared slightly derelict, unlike the bright metalwork of some zealous villages. It told him much about the place. 'I see this is not a flogging village.'

'The stocks are rarely used here. Before she died, there was an old crone always insisting I should sentence public punishments – I kept her in check with threats of calling in the Witch Finder!'

Both men were laughing as they strolled towards the Master House.

'Hadn't you better raise them?'

'Of course.' With outstretched arms, the Master signalled the people to their feet.

Then The Examiner saw her.

His journey had not been wasted; High Lord Sevolian would be more than pleased to add her to his collection of handmaidens. She was tall and slim-waisted, with the womanly outline his Lordship demanded. Those curves just had to be genuine; village women had no access to the black-market corsetry worn by their richer sisters in Sion, flouting religious law. (For it was written in the thirty-eighth Commandment: *Woman, thou shalt not tempt Man*.)

And those grey, penetrating eyes – so distinctive. Not pretty in the usual way. He had never seen a woman remotely like her.

He tried not to stare, but for a moment their eyes locked.

She smiled.

He found himself seated in the Master's study, a drink of the usual Moonsglow in his hand – he had no recollection of the intervening minute or so, just the knowledge that already she had somehow communicated her ... *essence* to him.

'You don't like her, do you?'

The Examiner realised he'd been frowning. It would do no harm to let him think that – it was amazing what revelations could be brought forth with a little pressure upon an anxious Master. 'Her face is not as pretty as other maids in his Lordship's household, and to be frank, her physique may be a little too ... well-developed for his tastes.'

'That's *not* what I heard! Apparently he likes them ...'

A warning glance let the Master know he was on dangerous ground. The Examiner eased his expression. 'I'll examine her of course,' he gestured dismissively, 'but are there any others?'

The Master paled. 'Well, Examiner, I would have thought ... Well, yes, there are a couple of other girls who come to mind, not exactly *petite* – but attractive young women, nevertheless. All of these girls have been on the Alpha education program for the last five summers – I'm sure at least one will measure up.'

He was beginning to sound desperate, terrified that the Examiner would return empty-handed to his Lord after a long, wasted journey.

'Can you provide a secure place where I can carry out the examinations without disturbance?'

The Master nodded. 'Certainly; right here in this study.'

'Thank you.' He looked at the worried old man and took pity. 'Let us see how your girls measure up.'

'You mean …?'

'Of course! You are very welcome to observe the examinations.'

The first girl was summoned within the hour. She had clear blue eyes and the delightful promise of a shapely figure under her best whites.

'Bless the Holy One!'

'May the Holy One be blessed, Master.'

Fifteen Eden summers, her file said; just over twenty standard years old, thought the Examiner. She would've been snapped up and married summers ago if the Disciple hadn't conscripted all the younger men for his crazy interstellar crusades. She looked up at him, bursting to find out the real meaning of all this. From that too-innocent look in those blue eyes, he thought she had a good idea already.

'You may rise,' said the Master. She arose with a rustle of linen. 'My guest has been sent by High Lord Sevolian himself!' Her mouth opened in awe.

The Examiner unfastened his case. The girl's mouth opened further as she saw the shallow crown with its diamonds, sapphires and emeralds. He carefully placed the glittering device on her head. She remained quite still, staring at him as if there were no one else in the world.

'I am the Examiner. The Master has gone and we are alone. You will only hear me when I talk directly to you. Do you understand?'

'Yes, sir.'

'Good. When I take the jewels off your head you will remember only a wonderful experience. I am going to ask you to do some unusual things, things you may never have done before. This concerns your oath of fealty. Do you remember your oath of fealty?'

'Certainly, sir; *Obey ye and follow in joy, without question or doubt, the orders and guidance of thy appointed Lords.*'

89

'Good. His Lordship requires me to examine you. Go behind that screen. You will find a chair and robe. Leave all your clothes on the chair and put on the robe.'

She went behind the screen.

'Great Lord! So *that* is the "Probe" … she will remember nothing?' the Master whispered.

'Only because I asked her.'

'My God! The ultimate control …'

'It is merely a tool, nothing "ultimate" about it! Like any tool it must be used with some care. The jewels are genuine. Electrodes stimulate hormonal flow and heighten suggestibility but the subject remains fully conscious as you can see. She cannot be made to do anything that is fundamentally disagreeable to her.'

She emerged in a short robe. The Master stared. Bare arms and thighs were rarely seen in his puritan society.

The Examiner was very calm. 'Come to me. Don't lower your eyes. Good. There is something you really want to do. You want to show me your body. It is quite all right; I would like to see it.'

After a slight pause, she gasped, 'Yes, sir, I really would.'

'Then hand me the robe.'

It was late morning in the long Eden day when Andromeda was summoned. She dropped to her knees at the sight of blue robes.

'Please stand.'

She stood and smiled that smile again. Close up, her physical presence was almost overwhelming, but the Examiner began his routine. Somehow it seemed crude and inappropriate for a woman like her. Now here she stood in the same robe that had briefly covered the other two girls, but he hesitated to bare her to the old man.

'Shouldn't she be nude by now?' said the Master, talkative with the Moonsglow, and the confidence that the

90

girls couldn't hear him. 'I can't wait to see her tits; they must be fantastic! Sevolian will be unable to resist them, I'll wager! After all this feeling and fooling around I'd like to see you actually spear this girl. Like to poke-in myself, for that matter, but his Lordship would have our balls for bangles, eh? Ha, ha!'

'We mustn't rush this one, Master.'

'Oh? Why not?'

'Remember, basically they must *want* to be examined, and the suggestion takes time to sink in. In this case I sense a reluctance.' It was a lie. He knew her feelings by the look she gave him. But she was special. He could not examine Andromeda with this drunk about to paw her. Something had to be done.

'Master, come a little closer to us, I want to try something.'

'Ha, ha, always, ready to try something … Hey, what are you …'

The Examiner swiftly removed the device from the woman's head and planted it on the Master's. The Master stood still, his head slightly tilted to one side, looking like some senile monarch.

'Master, you are feeling extremely tired. In a few moments you will sleep in your chair, and when you awake you will remember that we examined Andromeda exactly like the others. I let you touch her as much as you wished, and you were very pleased with her; she was exactly as you'd desired. Now sit down … that's good. You will now fall into a very deep sleep, and if I don't awake you earlier, you will sleep until the study clock chimes the sound of midnight.' He carefully removed the crown from the snoring head and put it to one side.

Andromeda was holding the thick sweep of dark hair where the device had rested. 'How do you feel?' he said with infinite kindness.

'I … I can't remember what I'm doing here … this robe

… I don't have anything on underneath …'

'You have a headache?'

'Yes, a bad one. I hardly ever have them.'

'I'm so sorry Andromeda; I had to quickly remove a machine that was on your head – a kind of hypnotic probe. The headache will fade in a few minutes.' He looked at her as he gathered his thoughts. She gazed straight back at him, trusting him.

'Andromeda, sit with me.'

They sat on the large sofa, away from the sleeping man. 'Listen carefully; I have much to say. I'm going to tell you many things about this world – the not-so-beautiful Eden – the real world outside this village and the way it is run. I'm going to tell you who controls it, and why I am here. This is all very dangerous knowledge – I am heavily involved with evil, the evil that wraps this planet like a cloak.'

Andromeda listened for more than a standard hour. Who was this tall, dangerous-looking visitor in his blue robes who spoke so well and openly to her? She began to find out. He seemed quite different to the few Holy Men she'd seen or knew of, such as the Master or the Disciple (whose picture hung in every dwelling-place on the planet). She hadn't realised that Holy Men could be so *young*. Before today – right up to the moment she had seen him dash youthfully out of his flying machine, there had been no other man for her other than Gareth, away on Crusade, but this intelligent, sophisticated man was in another league altogether.

He told her many things; about his mission, about the Probe and the other girls, about the High Lords and their harems of women; about the tyranny of the Disciple. Finally, and with obvious sensitivity, he told her of the lies and fairytales of the religion she'd grown up with. How it had been cynically patched together from the worst parts of old Earth's religions to enslave Eden, and now, through the

Crusades, to try and conquer other settled worlds and systems.

She understood it all. It had to be true. Instead of shattering her world, it made it real at last. The very basis of the life she had been taught to live was exposed as the sham she'd always suspected it to be.

She had to escape somehow, and this wonderful man was the key. 'Why do you tell me all this, Examiner?'

'Don't call me that. That is just my function. I'd rather you spoke my name.'

'What *is* your name?'

He hesitated. 'Call me John.'

'John, you are a fine man.'

He didn't answer. Perhaps he could tell that she was well on the way to loving him, as many women must have before her.

'What about the Master?' she asked, looking across to the old man.

'I have sent him into a deep sleep with the probe … he won't even know that it was used on him.' The Examiner shook his head. He looked so unhappy.

She stretched a comforting arm around his broad back. 'So you will leave me here and return empty-handed to High Lord Sevolian?' As he nodded she came to a decision. Thoughts of Gareth had long faded from her mind. 'Examine me as you did the others. You will not need the probe – I want to have the memory of the experience. Let me remember what you did and then take me with you to Sevolian's castle. I'll take my chances there – I can't stay here any longer.'

A loud peal of thunder broke overhead and rumbled slowly away into the distance. A heavy drumming began. The afternoon rains had arrived early. They sat in silence for a while.

'Very well, Andromeda, we'll begin your examination…'

He stood, and she rose to face him.

'At this point I ask if you would like to ...' he felt ludicrously embarrassed.

A wry smile crossed her face. 'Take off this robe?' She opened it and let it slip from her shoulders to the floor. From vast experience he knew how she would look, and yet the actual sight of her body aroused him deeply. Womanly perfection. Her pointing nipples (just a little darker and larger than he had imagined) held out high, breasts swinging slightly as she breathed. He could never allow another man's hand to touch this piece of heaven.

'I suppose now you feel my breasts?' She was smiling, aware of her power, swaying her body slightly.

'I *measure* you next Andromeda, so please stand still,' he said thickly. He fumbled with the recorder like an inexperienced boy. He gently pressed it over the creamy white flesh of her breasts, over each nipple that firmed with its contact, and into the deep valley between.

'Couldn't you get my size and form from a holovid of me?'

'How do you know of holovids?'

'Whispers, underground talk ... other villages must be the same, surely?'

'The 'vid comes later, but it doesn't measure ...' He was absurdly embarrassed again.

'Softness,' she supplied, pushing her left breast deep into his hands. He felt yielding firmness, his long fingers cupping automatically around her flesh, her nipple pushing hard against his palm. He almost lost control with his wish to suck and bite that dark focus of his desire. He felt his body stiffen and rise in anticipation of a service an Examiner was forbidden to perform. The hardness was uncomfortably restrained by his robes.

As he let go of the squeezed breast, the white finger-marks persisted around the dark central disc. Both breasts seemed to look at him like big brown eyes. Her real, grey

94

eyes held him for a second before their mouths and bodies came together. He gripped her waist. Their tongues met. His hands slipped lower, sliding over the skin of her hips, squeezing the cheeks of her buttocks. He pulled back abruptly.

'Andromeda,' he said harshly, 'Have you had lovers?' The bad question was deliberate. With a lesser woman it would have killed the sex there and then, bringing back memories and past promises.

'Oh, John … Not as you would define it, no. I was betrothed to a boy away on the Crusades …'

'Was? Your file says you *are* betrothed.' His voice was still harsh.

'Not after today.' Looking up into his eyes she moved against him, pressing her body against the hard outline she could clearly feel through his robe. 'I knew there would be a file. What else does it say?'

'It says that you are highly intelligent – the brightest person in the village, in fact.'

'That is hardly a compliment in *this* village!' Her hands slipped under his robes and closed around him, feeling his length. The rains were drumming harder on the roof as he let her free him from his cloth. Soon he stood as naked as she. Her touch was delicious. He saw her frightened look as she gently cradled the dangerous weapon in her hands. Despite her great boldness she was inexperienced. She lightly traced a finger around the taut, curving head. Her mouth opened in a soft gasp. 'John, you are so big; how can you go inside me?'

'I must *not* go inside you, Andromeda.'

It would be the end for both of them if Sevolian ever found out, he explained.

'Unless you took me for wife?'

'You *are* desperate to escape this village!'

'No. I want you, and I want to leave this prison.' She squatted down. Very deliberately, she drew the head of his penis up to her mouth, kissed the glistening tip while laying the shaft along her right breast. As her lips enveloped him he cradled her breast, pushing its projecting nipple under his sac, against the very root of his shaft where it curved up into his body.

There was a change in the room; the drone of conversation had stopped, leaving only the subdued roar of the rain. Then the Study clock slowly chimed the fourteen strokes of noon – or midnight. He was so tired, but this was the signal he must obey. He opened his eyes. He saw the woman. He remembered how the Examiner had let him handle her delicious body.

He saw her long bare back with the cascading hair dark upon it, her slim waist and broad heart-shaped bottom as she knelt before the naked man. Her left breast was pushed out sideways by his thigh ... the man's hanging fingers were stroking the standing nipple ... she was sucking on him.

The sex began and there was no turning back. She'd experimented a little with Gareth, so this was not quite her first time.

She drank the early fluid that oozed deep into her mouth as he gently explored her breasts, her thighs, her buttocks and the folds between. She began to moan. Eventually, she pulled her lips away, sucking and licking the tip as another drop welled out. She ran it along her lips with her tongue as she fixed her grey eyes on his. 'Now fuck me, John,' she whispered.

She had released him. By the Disciple! He caught a fantastic glimpse of her as she turned, dropping onto her hands and knees, hair cascading forward, now hiding the tips of her magnificent tits as they brushed the carpet. The Examiner had seized her offered up buttocks and was lining up his long cock to take her from behind.

He spread her bottom wide and engaged the head against her inner lips. He held still for a moment as she squirmed and rolled to sit back on the tip of him.

Then he moved. She cried out as he began to penetrate her. The cry faded to a long moan of pleasure. She was tight but smoothly yielding as his shaft slid slowly in. He could feel the muscle mass of each buttock separating as he pushed in deeper.

He shimmied her bottom with his hands and she began rolling it around his shaft, allowing him to slip in even further. He felt gently under her lips and caressed the flesh that rose to his fingertips. She was moaning again as she finally filled to her limit.

Then he began his long deep strokes, grasping her buttocks, her waist, her big swinging breasts as they came to hand. Her head was way down as he rode her hard; she seemed to be watching his hanging sac slapping against her. On and on he went, until her moans became more urgent cries.

As she began her climax, she reached back and held him. He tried to hold back, but the howling, bucking woman milking him would not be denied. The first full ejaculation leapt from him. Her squirming, rolling buttocks began a faster motion, and every few seconds another spurt shot into her. She cried out as he kept thrusting deep, the semen finally overflowing, running down the inside of her legs.

They were still locked together when the Master joined them. In disbelief John saw him grasp and knead the glistening globes of Andromeda's hanging breasts, slap and smack her buttocks.

'*My* turn now Brother! Let *me* ride the bitch!'

Andromeda felt the extra hands on her body and began to scream. The Master recoiled; probably amazed he was no longer invisible to the woman.

John's first impulse was to kill. Instead he grabbed the jewelled crown and planted it hard on the Master's head.

The trees dropped away below, churning from the gale of lift-off.

'John, I still don't understand.'

'What don't you understand?' Their voices were raised against the roar of the rotors. The roaring diminished somewhat as he transitioned to forward flight. He briefly glanced sideways to see her expression. 'Why I gave him those jewels from the probe? It cannot erase the memory of something he saw when not wearing it – I had to buy his silence.'

'No, I understand bribery and blackmail, but how are you going to explain the loss to Lord Sevolian?'

'Those stones are there for many contingencies. I'm not just examining women, I find out a lot about the Master and his village.'

'I see. So the Master has failed a test?'

'No, not at all. I can see that he runs the village reasonably well. He's not cruel, just greedy. The *real* test will be when I see how he spends his new-found wealth.'

She thought for a moment as the craft settled into cruising flight. 'Will I be able to see you at the Castle?'

'From time to time we should glimpse one another, but I have a heavy schedule of work. This may be the last time we are together in total privacy.' He switched the autopilot to Command Mode, and after a quick glance around the panel he turned his full attention to her. 'You can unbuckle now.'

He led her to the luxurious padded area behind the flight seats. It was much quieter back here. They could look out on the endless forest passing far below.

She kissed him as he opened her clothes and released her breasts into his hands. Soon the lovers were naked and he was slipping deep inside her body again.

When he was totally her master and she fully his mistress, she asked him, 'Who are you, John?'

'I am the Examiner.'

'Yes I know, but you're more than that.'

She will never disappoint me, he thought. 'You *are* smart, Andromeda.'

'By the Disciple! You! You're Sevolian, aren't you?'

He smiled.

The Lady And The Highwayman
by Charlotte Wickham

Lady Amelia Farley chuckled to herself, the sound of Lightning's hooves thundering in her ears, as they got further and further away from the stifling confines of Farley Hall.

"I forbid you to ride that horse again, Amelia!" Her father's voice had boomed at breakfast when he had found out that his daughter had disobeyed him again. "If you must ride, then I urge you to ride like the lady you are and go on a gentle trot on Lizzie or any other of the placid ponies which I've bought especially for you. It won't do for anyone to see Lady Amelia Farley riding like a ruffian on a wild stallion. Think of your reputation, girl! You'll never marry, if you insist on behaving in such an obscene manner."

Lord Farley would much rather his elder daughter behaved like her younger sister, Arabella, and occupied her time with ladylike pursuits like embroidery, needlework and crochet, however, the thought of spending another minute pricking her thumbs and pacing the sitting room was enough to drive Amelia mad! She yearned for wide open spaces, the fresh country air and the freedom to do what she liked, when she liked. So, when she spotted her mother dozing in the conservatory, she escaped to the stables and, after checking that the stable hands weren't around, she saddled up Lightning and rode as far away from Farley Hall as she possibly could!

When the news that she had once again behaved so improperly reached her parents' ears, Amelia knew that her father would be furious and that her mother would be upset and disappointed, but Amelia was tired of being held captive in her own home, and although she knew that on her return home she would have to face the consequences of her actions, for now, she'd just take pleasure in the fact that she was her own woman, free to do what she liked for the next couple of hours.

"Isn't this wonderful, Lightning?" Amelia stroked the horse's neck and jumped off, leading the horse to the nearby lake. "Why would anyone want to spend their days locked in a stuffy room when they could be enjoying all this beauty?"

"Why indeed?" She heard a deep masculine voice mutter behind her.

Amelia stopped in her tracks, her eyes widening with fear. She hadn't been expecting company – and she certainly hadn't been expecting male company!

She took a deep breath and kept her back to him, hoping that her uninvited guest might take the hint and leave her alone. But, when she felt the cold circumference of a steel pistol against the back of her neck, Amelia let out a cry of pain.

"W-What do you want from me?" She trembled, her voice cracking with fear and panic. She could feel his hands running up and down her spine, his musky scent filling her nostrils. "Please don't hurt me."

She heard him chuckle from behind her, a deep, throaty chortle that made her knees shake. "You do as I say, Lady Farley, and nobody gets hurt."

"Lady Farley? B-But how do you know my name?" Amelia asked her captor, trying not to flinch when she felt his hands caress her buttocks.

He spun her round to face him, penetrating blue eyes clashing deviously with hers. "I know all there is to know about you and your family, Lady Farley." He muttered, as he pulled her towards him, his shaft rubbing insistently against her belly while his strong hands cupped her buttocks and then proceeded to spank them lightly with glee. "I wouldn't be much of a highwayman if I didn't know that you were the elder daughter of the richest man in the county."

"What is it that you want from me?" She asked him again, her eyes wide with fear and desire. She had always thought that highwaymen were ghastly creatures with long greasy hair and untidy whiskers, who wore patched clothes and muddy boots – she certainly never envisaged that they'd be tall, tawny-haired and as handsome as sin!

Amelia's gaze slid down his face and took in his broad masculine shoulders, muscular chest and narrow waist, encased in a long black overcoat, a white shirt and skin-tight pantaloons which emphasized the strength of his huge thighs – and the size of his bulging erection!

"Like what you see, do you, Lady Farley?" he growled, his fingers caressing her spine. "I bet this is the first time in your life you've come this close to a real man."

"Let me go!" Amelia insisted, even though every cell in her body seemed to be surrendering to his touch.

"I give the orders around here, my lady," he mocked her, as he captured her lips with his own.

Amelia's fingers curled into fists and pounded against his hard chest, but the highwayman wasn't going to let his prey get away from him so easily!

His teeth bit down on her lower lip and her mouth dropped open in shock, allowing him to gain entrance and to swoop in and invade her mouth. His tongue sought out hers and he gently began to coax her and caress her in a cruel yet decadent game of passion where they both emerged victorious.

Amelia couldn't believe that she had succumbed to this common man who would doubtlessly ruin her reputation! But as his lips began to slide down the smooth column of her throat and lick a trail of fire down her neck, she found herself unable to care about her reputation, her family or what anyone passing might say about her scandalous behaviour in broad daylight with a man she had never met, and instead prepared herself to succumb to her captor's touch.

Amelia felt his strong hands cup her breasts and his fingers skimming her erect nipples through the fabric of her dress. She let out a small scream as he tore her bodice and got rid of the barrier of clothing between his hands and her breasts.

"You've got wonderful tits, my lady." He exclaimed, his tongue curling round a rigid aureole and his teeth gently nibbling the tight bud.

Amelia's back arched with absolute pleasure, her hands tearing away at the coat he was wearing. She wanted to see her highwayman naked. She wanted to feast her eyes on the perfect body hidden between the folds of his clothing and touch him and caress him in the same delicious way.

His lips still clamped on her nipples, he got rid of his coat and shirt, and Amelia's mouth dried up as she saw his powerful torso inches away from her face. With shaking hands, she caressed his shoulders and slid her hand down his strong back.

"That feels so good, sweetheart," he growled, when her hands couldn't resist stroking his tight backside. "Feel what you're doing to me, Lady Farley," he cried, grabbing her hand and putting her fist onto his bulging erection.

Amelia's eyes widened with amazement as she felt his cock pulsating between her fingers. She couldn't believe that she was the reason for his ardent arousal. The men she usually came into contact with had made it quite clear that the only thing they had found desirable about her was her fortune; she couldn't countenance the fact that a complete stranger could be driven to such lengths of ecstasy by the sight of her naked breasts!

Her fingers impatient to feel him, she undid the buttons of his pantaloons and reached for his erection, her eyes unable to believe just how big he was! When her fingers curled around his cock and began to slide up and down the length of his impressive shaft, Amelia could hear him moaning with pleasure. She took him into her mouth, her tongue licking the head and swooping over the eye and down the underside. She could hear his breathing growing shallower, his cries of passion escalating and his need for her expanding with every lick of her tongue.

"I need to come inside you!" he yelled, as he pulled her up and tore at her dress. Seeing her naked pussy glistening with moistness in front of him only served to make him harder. As his tongue traced the outline of her labia majora and began to lap up the liquid shimmering on her pussy, his lips sought out her clitoris and began to suck it impatiently.

He could feel her hands tugging at his hair and pushing his face deeper and deeper into her womanhood. When he felt that he would explode if he didn't fuck her, he replaced his mouth with his cock and he thrust into her, pounding harder and harder inside her until she screamed when she reached an earth-shattering climax.

Seeing her face contorting with absolute pleasure made him even harder than he was already, so he thrust deeper and deeper inside of her; sliding his rod in and out of her pussy and increasing his strokes with every push, until he felt his thick, creamy seed spilling inside her pussy.

"I certainly got more than I bargained for," he whispered, still lying inside her as his hands stroked her breasts.

"You never said what you wanted from me," Amelia said, snaking her legs around his waist, keeping him captive inside her. "I still cannot imagine what you could possibly have taken from me. I've got no money or jewellery; it's just me and Lightning."

Her highwayman smiled. "Ah, my lady, but that horse is worth its weight in gold. Had I managed to abscond with him, I'd have ended up a very rich man."

Amelia chuckled, as she pushed herself up on her elbows and placed a tender kiss on his lips.

Her highwayman was just about to deepen their kiss, when suddenly the sound of a horse's hooves pounding through the air echoed through the woods. Aware that if he was caught with a naked Amelia he would be hanged, he gathered his clothes, and pulling her once more towards him, kissed her tenderly and said, "I'm sorry about this, my lady. I didn't mean to hurt you. I hope that we will meet again."

And he disappeared into the distance, leaving a shocked Amelia clutching her torn dress to her naked body, yearning to feel his touch upon hers once more.

A month had passed since that fateful day and she still hadn't managed to forget her passionate encounter with her tawny-haired adventurer.

She had spent night after night tossing and turning in her bed, remembering his naked body and yearning to feel his skin under her fingertips, his lips on hers and his tongue arousing every single nerve in her body. Every night, she would wonder what he was doing and whether he remembered her with the same frequency which she remembered him.

Luckily, her parents had believed the story she had told them when one of the stable boys had found her naked, clutching her tattered garments and weeping with the loss of her lover, whom she doubted she would ever see again.

"I told you not to be so foolish!" Her father had screamed at her, unaware of the true reason behind his daughter's tears. "Now, look what has happened. You were lucky, my girl, that you weren't raped and left for dead!"

But Amelia didn't see much point in carrying on; not if it meant that she would spend the rest of her life yearning for the one man she knew she could never have.

"Now, do look sharp, my dear," her mother's whining voice interrupted her thoughts. "Who knows, maybe at Lady Merrick's ball you'll finally meet a gentleman who will whisk you off your feet!"

Amelia smiled weakly, knowing full well that she would be spending the evening chatting away to decrepit old dowagers and listening to avaricious younger sons making empty promises to her in order to get their hands on her fortune.

When Amelia and her mother entered the ballroom, they were greeted by Lady Merrick, who seemed to be particularly excited about something.

"Oh, you've come finally!" She exclaimed, her ample bosom heaving with excitement. "Amelia, my darling, I'd like you to meet my nephew, Tristan Maddox. He's just come down from Cambridge and he can't wait to meet you."

Amelia pasted onto her face a welcoming smile, but when she turned round and spotted Tristan Maddox, her mouth dropped open and her jaw hit the floor.

It was her highwayman! With his tawny curls tamed and wearing the season's fashions, he looked like any other respectable gentleman of good breeding!

"Lady Farley," his voice sent shivers of pleasure racing up and down her spine. "I've been so looking forward to meeting you. Something tells me that the two of us will be great friends."

And he kissed the back of her hand, his tongue running over her knuckles; a deliciously sensual prelude to all the delights he had in store for her in the future.

The Treat
by Amelia Flint

Something about big, luxurious houses has always got me going. All those rich, opulent textures: the silk curtains, the satin bedsheets, the velvet upholstery ... sheer delight. I can't help it, all that opulence, all that *wealth* just makes me feel damp and excited. One of my favourite fantasies is being fucked by an old man who is just filthy, *filthy* rich – his stubby fingers loaded with gold rings squeezing my red nipples as he blindfolds me and gags me with ropes made of crisp ten-pound notes. Sometimes I imagine him getting me off with a coin – rubbing its smooth, rounded edge against my clit until I come, hard, coating the Queen's face with my excitement.

Call me shallow, call me whatever you like – who can deny that money is an aphrodisiac? Unfortunately, I don't have a lot of it myself. And that's why working for the Farringtons in their palatial home, a sprawling estate near London, proved to be the perfect job. I cleaned their house, and while I was doing it I routinely got myself off on the *lavishness* of my surroundings. While they commended me for my excellent laundering abilities, and paid me an hourly wage, I brought myself off on the edge of their gold brocade curtains – in their bubble-jet Jacuzzi – *anywhere*, my eager fingers stimulating my throbbing clit as I thought about Mr Farrington's yearly income. The opportunity for giving myself the occasional treat was just too good to miss out on. And doesn't a cleaning lady deserve a little treat now and again?

The Farringtons were frightfully posh. They could have passed for Camilla and Charles, with their far back accents and identical braying laughs. Mrs Farrington was an uptight fusspot who wore her make-up like army paint, and always had coral lipstick smeared on her protruding front teeth. Her husband was fat, middle aged, and was just about clinging on to what was left of his hair. I'm no oil painting and I'm fairly certain that they didn't hire me for my looks – '*sturdy*,' Mrs F. liked to describe me as – but more than once I caught him eyeing up my plump breasts and rear, constrained in the ridiculous starched uniform they insisted I wear. He'd let his gaze linger on me, sometimes in full view of his oblivious wife, and I didn't have to be a mind reader to know that he was imagining what I'd look like naked.

On this particular day, Mrs Farrington stood there, giving me the day's orders. 'Clean the mirrors with *vinegar*, dear, nothing less will do. We want them to *sparkle*, don't we?'

I nodded in agreement as she continued, hiding my irritation with her fussy, elaborate instructions, and resisting the urge to tell her that I'd do a hell of a lot better job if she just left me to it. But I held my tongue, and eventually she finished and made off for her ladies luncheon. I breathed a sigh of relief. I had the house to myself now, just the way I wanted it.

A morning of dusting, vacuuming and laundry had me sweating and tired. I was looking forward to my 'treat' at the end of the day more than usual. I knew exactly where I was going to have it – in the master bedroom. I hadn't dared before, but I was annoyed after Mrs Farrington's pernickety orders that morning, and my treats had been a little stale of late. The whole procedure needed livening up.

Late afternoon, when most of the chores had been completed, but early enough so that there was no chance of discovery, I slipped into the master bedroom. My nipples stiffened just walking through the door, as I contemplated what I was about to do.

I sat on the bed, and started out as I always did – smoothing the sheets with the flat of my hand, breathing in deeply, running my hands over the restricting uniform that held my curves. The bed was opposite a huge mirror that stretched the whole expanse of one wall. I could feel myself getting damp already as I thought about how much more fun the treat would be if I could watch myself administering it.

My nipples chafed against the rigid uniform as I leaned down to pulled my tights off and step out of my panties. It was just as well, discarding them; my growing excitement had spread in a dark stain through the lace, and had settled in shining traces on my hefty thighs. I heaved myself back onto the bed and spread my legs slowly in front of the mirror, the moist pink purse of my sex revealed in all its glory. The long slit of my labia was wet and curved in a smile as it waited expectantly to be loved by my hand.

I may not be a looker, as such, but I do pride myself on having a very pretty pussy. I splayed it with my fingers now, holding each slick lip apart so that the gleaming swell of my clitoris was reflected in the mirror. I looked at it for a few moments, smiling with satisfaction at the image of myself, legs akimbo, cunt splayed over the lacy eiderdowns that Mrs Farrington favoured. I imagined the juice from my cunt dripping onto the lace, leaving tell-tale little stains, and how Mrs Farrington might set me to work the next day scrubbing the smears of my own arousal from her linen. The thought made my clit pulse and, all of a sudden, I couldn't help but touch the little bud with my fingertips.

It swelled at my touch, immediately. I lay back, arching my back and tilting my hips to heighten the sensation, and my eye was caught by the feather duster I'd discarded earlier, sitting beside me. In a moment of inspiration, I grabbed it. I ran the smooth feathers through my fingers for a few moments, the nerves in my fingertips thrilling at the lightness of the touch. Then, I moved the duster lower, sweeping the feathers over my stomach towards the hot, wet, expectant cavern of my pussy.

My clit convulsed as the feathers brushed it – the whisper-soft touch tantalized me so much that my cunt threatened to give itself up to orgasm then and there – but I was determined to hold it off until the last possible moment.

I started to fuck myself with the end of the duster. It wasn't thick enough, not really, but my hungry pussy welcomed the insertion of something hard and unyielding, the slippery walls clenching around it with each sharp thrust. Just as I was reaching down to rub the white-hot nub of my clit in time to the self-made thrusting motions, a small half-cough from the doorway stopped me dead in my tracks. My heart leaped into my throat as I froze in panic.

Mr Farrington. He had entered the room behind me, but I could see him in the mirror. He was clutching a briefcase, and had stopped midway through the action of unknotting his tie. He, too, had frozen in shock.

What a strange tableau we made. The businessman, about to change out of his suit after coming home early from work. The slutty cleaner, eyes glazed with excitement, busy hands now stilled between her legs. A duster rammed deep into her cunt and her excitement leaking out of her into sticky pools on the bedspread. Jesus. A slow, searing burn of humiliation spread slowly over my neck and face. Tears of embarrassment sprang to my eyes. I would be sacked, I would lose my job and reputation.

And yet, my treacherous pussy twitched. The shock of discovery was horrifying, but somehow my humiliation didn't stretch to my nether regions and they spasmed excitedly under the gaze of Mr Farrington.

I pulled the duster from between my legs with an agonizing slurp, and opened my mouth to begin grovelling and apologising.

'Don't stop,' he said, in a strangled voice. The filthy old man. I should have known that he would love this. My panic and mortification began to recede as my nether regions convulsed once again.

He came into the room and shut the door behind him, but didn't come any closer to me. He dropped his briefcase on the floor. His eyes were bulging, a vein popped in his forehead, and his flabby cheeks were slowly turning purple. The jowls beneath his chin started to quiver slightly. I lowered my eyes to his crotch, and saw that, beneath the expensive material of the suit, his cock was straining, sticking out like a flagpole.

Unbidden, an image of his naked cock popped into my head. Short, squat, and tree-trunk thick it would be, with sparse grey hairs sprouting about the base and the foreskin thick and fleshy. I thought about being fucked by Mr Farrington's meaty weapon, the dull pink shaft threaded with broken veins sliding in and out of me while I bounced in his lap, my pendulous breasts swinging in his face and my beefy thighs gripping him tight. I thought about Mrs Farrington watching, her coral-lipsticked mouth open in an O as she watched our diabolical screwing.

Suddenly his instruction, '*don't stop*,' became impossible *not* to follow. I turned my gaze back to the flushed, aroused version of myself in the mirror. Aware of Mr Farrington's reflected eyes on me, tentatively I touched my finger to my clit again. The second it made contact my clit throbbed and my nipples stiffened against the starched uniform. God, that felt good. Wanting to explore the sensation further, I used my left hand to work my nipple through the thick material, the muffled intake of breath from the corner behind me spurring me on.

With one hand, I squeezed the hardened peak of my

nipple, manipulating it as much as the uniform would allow. With the other, I massaged my clit, my engorged pussy walls clamouring to be penetrated as swells of excitement pulsated through my sopping cunt. I felt as though my nipples and clit were connected by ropes of fire – the sensation of my merciless fingers on both was sending feverish flashes through my nervous system.

I slid my eyes sideways to watch Mr Farrington watching me. His pupils were dilated, his face puce, and he was wheezing like an asthmatic running up a hill. The shock of finding me *in flagrante* had faded for us both now, and his eyes were fixated on my dripping, distended hole, watching my slippery fingers flicking away at the bleeding cherry of my clit.

To my delight, he began to unbutton his fly, his fingers trembling and fumbling so much that each button came undone slowly. As he started to ease his cock out I masturbated myself more quickly, anticipation of seeing it flooding through me. He drew it from the folds of his trousers at last and I sighed. It looked much as I had expected – a little longer, the blood beating through it angrily, the swollen flushed head crowned with a sticky gleam of moisture. A smell of sex began to permeate the room as our exposed organs, separated by several feet of distance, pulsed their heady scent into the air. It mingled with the pot-pourri Mrs F. favoured, and I smiled at the thought of her breathing in the fuck-smell hanging in the air as she laid her head down to sleep that evening.

I spread my pussy as wide as it would go, the milk flowing from it smearing my thighs and making it difficult to keep my fingers in place. The tremors in my groin were coming thick and fast now, and as Mr Farrington started to roughly wank his cock in time with my own motions I determined to put on the best display he'd ever seen while getting myself off all over Mrs F.'s bed.

Our eyes still locked on each other through the mirror, I

gave myself up to the sensation my hands were causing, and rubbed at my clit so hard that the first waves of orgasm began to pulse through me. Mr Farrington gave a strangled moan. The image of being fucked by a rich man came back to me and I closed my eyes, imagining myself impaled on his cock.

Writhing with pleasure, but needing something to heighten it even further, I grasped the feather duster once again and wet it using my cunt before reaching round to slip it into my anus. Being so thin, it hardly met any resistance as I pushed it into the tight flesh, the lube from my pussy helping it slide in easily. Nevertheless, the contact it made with the nerves in my arse was explosive as the feeling merged with the orgasm building on the end of my fingers, finally causing a cascade of hot ecstasy to flow through me. As I came, thrashing on the lace eiderdown, my arse clenching like mad over the end of the duster, Mr Farrington let out an inarticulate cry and milked himself to orgasm. His hand on his thick cock was a blur, and blood vessels threatened to explode in his face. The spunk arced gracefully out of the straining split at the head of his organ, and splattered across the plush carpet.

When my pulse had slowed and my heavy breathing had subsided, I sat up and arranged my clothes, my raw cunt twitching as I pulled my cold, wet panties back on.

'I'm so sorry, Mr Farrington,' I said with my customary politeness. 'I'll get all this mess taken care of immediately.'

He could barely look me in the eye, but grunted acknowledgement and tucked his penis, now flaccid, back into his trousers. As he made his way into the double-ensuite, I picked up the sticky duster and began to lightly flick it over the furniture, my nipples still tight and my clit tingling with the excitement of what had taken place.

I cleaned the end of the duster, put the vacuum away, and set about finishing the day's work. The thrill of touching myself in that gorgeous, spacious room with Mrs

F's husband masturbating in front of me, went through me again and again. The treat hadn't turned out as it usually did. But then I always liked a little variation in my routine.

The Key
by Jim Baker

Don woke slowly. He shook his head, stretched his arms wide, and opened his eyes as his fingers brushed against the warm body in the bed beside him.

He lifted the sheet and feasted his eyes on Sally's firm round breasts. He bent and took a nipple between his lips, running his tongue around the flesh as it stiffened.

She came awake, yawning and stretching, and then sighed with pleasure as his fingers stroked her thighs. Her hand crept down and explored his stiff cock.

"My lord and master wants *more*? After last night?"

"It's Sunday morning. All married couples make love on Sunday mornings. It's the law."

"Well, we mustn't break the law. How would you like me, my lord?"

"On your knees, wench!"

She laughed, rolled on to her stomach and knelt facing the end of the bed, with her buttocks thrust high. They had been married for only six months, and their hunger for each other's bodies hadn't lessened one iota in that time.

Don settled behind her and guided the tip of his cock between the soft pink lips. Her flesh was slick from their lovemaking the night before and he slid into her easily.

He placed his hands lightly on her waist, luxuriated in the feel of the hot, tight flesh and began to thrust in and out

115

slowly, his eyes closed.

"Faster, Don!"

She forced her buttocks back against him.

"Oh sweetheart, it's starting already." She panted out the words. "Touch me, baby, please touch me now!"

He slid his hand under her. She screamed as his finger found her swollen clit and he opened his eyes – and screamed himself at the sight of a small, skeletal figure standing at the end of the bed. Teeth grinned obscenely in its fleshless skull. Its hand was raised, and a bony finger was raised high.

His head spun and he fell backward, his erection shrivelling away.

"Don, are you all right?" Sally squeezed his hand as she sat beside him, her face white and scared.

"It was like a kid!" Don croaked the words as he lay shivering on the bed.

"A kid?"

"At the end of the bed. It was a like dead child, a skeleton. It pointed its finger at us. You must have seen it!"

Sally put her arms around him.

"Hush, love. I had my eyes closed. Did you have a bad dream last night? You woke me up with all your thrashing about."

"Well, I did have a nightmare," Don admitted. He had stopped shivering but the picture of the ghastly figure stayed in his mind's eye.

"It was a memory from your dream, sweetheart, it wasn't real. Let me take your mind off it."

She took his cock between her fingers and played with it, her teeth nibbling at his ear. "Let's see if I can get our friend working again," she whispered.

Don body warmed as a feeling of arousal spread through it, and his cock grew in her hand. She ran a fingernail across the slit and a pearl of pre-come formed. She flicked it off with the tip of her tongue, and took the head into her mouth. Sucking gently, she ran her tongue round and round the swollen flesh until he was fully erect, and then slid back up the bed and planted a sloppy kiss on his lips.

"I want you back inside me," she whispered. She rolled over, and pulled him on top of her. Her legs clamped high around his back as he slid into her.

"Quickly, Don, quickly!"

Her body arched up to his as he began to thrust with long, steady strokes. "Faster, baby, faster!" Don increased the pace as her voice panted in his ear and the bedsprings creaked as he rammed into her. "Hard, Don, really hard! Harder!"

She moaned, and dug her nails into his shoulders, urging him on, writhing under him, and Don became lost in a world where there was nothing but the feel of his cock pounding in her hot flesh and the orgasm that was getting rapidly closer.

"Oh, Christ, Don … I'm going to come again!" Sally's nails dug into his back.

She gave a long, ecstatic scream and Don came in a blinding flash of pleasure, pumping frantically inside her. His climax seemed to go for ever – jet after jet spurted from his cock until he collapsed, spent.

She propped herself on one elbow and looked down at him.

"Wow! That was one of the best ever. I bet that made you forget the monster."

She got up and pulled on her dressing gown. "I'll make some tea."

Don smiled but the word *monster* had made him feel cold again, and he shivered.

On Monday morning the sunshine was streaming through the kitchen window as Sally
washed the dishes.

Don had been quiet through Sunday afternoon, but seemed to have shaken off his disquiet by dinner time. They had shared a bottle of wine and gone to bed early, dropping off to sleep almost immediately.

The ghostly figure had not been mentioned again.

Sally had awoken at seven o'clock to find her husband naked beside her, lying on his back with a huge erection. She slipped out of bed, found a bottle of baby oil and anointed the long rod of flesh. Then she lay back down beside him and watched his face as she gave him slow, gentle hand-job.

His eyes opened and he stared blearily at her.

"Hello, darling," she whispered. "Having a nice dream?"

Before he could reply she swung a long leg across his waist, straddled him and lowered herself on to his cock. He came wide awake very quickly as she rode him to a gloriously sticky climax.

Now it was ten o'clock, and she had the house to clean before taking Jack, their cocker spaniel, for a walk. He was sprawled under the kitchen table, watching her every move.

Sally pulled the plug, turned on the cold tap and stared in surprise as the running water revealed a large, rusty key beneath the remaining soapsuds.

She reached into the sink and picked it up, quite sure she had never seen it before. She bent down and held it out to Jack. "What's this, Jacky?"

The little dog stretched his nose forward, and sniffed. Then he backed away, stiff-legged. Sally watched in amazement as he bared his teeth, growled deep in his throat, and slunk out of the kitchen. She dropped the key and ran after him. He was huddled under a coffee table, quivering. She called him and eventually he crept out and relaxed as she petted him. She sat with him for a while, then went back to the kitchen, picked up the key and dropped it into the cutlery drawer.

When Don arrived home, she questioned him about it.

"Don, did you leave a key in the kitchen last night or this morning?"

"No. Have you lost one?"

"No, I found one."

She told him what had happened and he looked at her quizzically.

"You found a key in the washing up and it scared the dog. Been at the cooking sherry?"

"No! If you don't believe me, see for yourself. It's in the cutlery drawer."

Don went into the kitchen and returned immediately with the key in his hand.

"Where did you say you left it?"

"In the cutlery drawer."

"You *must* have been on the sherry. It was on the kitchen table."

Sally looked at him in disbelief.

"Don, I put it in the drawer this morning. It can't have been on the table."

He shook his head and started to laugh when the expression on her face stopped him. "Okay, love," he said. "It's only a key. It can't hurt you."

"I don't like it, Don. Get rid of it."

Don walked out of the back door and tossed the key into the dustbin.

"There, it's gone. Funny though, I think I know what it was for."

"What?"

"The shed."

Their converted cottage had a garden, at the bottom of which stood an old wooden shed.

"The shed? But surely that's got a padlock on it?"

"It has. But there's an old lock on the door as well. Come and see."

They walked out into the warm summer evening, and down to the black shed.

"There."

Sally saw the lock in the door, painted over with the

119

same black paint that covered the shed. Long disused, it had been replaced by a hasp and padlock.

"I reckon that old key belongs to it," he said.

As they started back to the house Sally took his hand in hers. "Don? Would you mind if we eat a bit late tonight?"

"I don't mind. Why?"

"I'd like to stay outside in the sun for a bit. I'll get some wine."

She went back to the house; Don turned and ran his fingers over the lock. Suddenly he felt cold, and the sunshine seemed paler. Then the feeling evaporated as he heard Sally's voice. She was carrying an open bottle of wine and two glasses, and a blanket was draped across her shoulder.

"Come on," she called. "Help me spread the blanket."

"Blanket? What's wrong with the garden chairs?"

"Oh, don't be stuffy. You used to enjoy the blanket before we got married. Or are you getting too old?"

She dropped the blanket and poured two glasses of wine.

"Cheeky. I'm not too old to give you six of the best on your pretty little backside."

"Promises, promises."

Sally drank half her wine, dropped to her knees and straightened the blanket.

Don held out his hand. "Let me top you up."

Sally gave him her glass and then squealed as he dropped down beside her, grabbed her and turned her face down across his knees.

"Too old, eh?"

He tugged her skirt up around her waist. "Silk panties, no less. Right, two with them on, and four with them off."

"You wouldn't!"

"Oh no?"

He spanked her lightly, just once on each silk-covered cheek.

Sally squealed, and wriggled frantically as he hooked his

120

fingers under the waistband and slid the panties down.

"Lovely," he whispered. She tensed as he caressed her with the palm of his hand and then screeched with indignation as it fell sharply, twice on each of the firm, round globes of flesh.

She began to struggle, and then stopped as his hand moved down between her legs and a fingertip found her clitoris.

The spanking had already excited her, and very soon her hips were jerking across his knees until she came to a shuddering climax. He held her until her body stopped shaking, pulled her pants up, smoothed down her skirt and let her go. She rolled away and lay on her back. Her hair was dishevelled and her eyes were shining.

"Nice?"

"Fantastic!" She stretched up her arms.

Don lay down, put his arms around her and as they kissed Sally worked her hand down and freed his rigid cock.

She took the shaft in one hand and ran the tip of the index finger of the other up and down the glans, making him shudder.

"So hard," she murmured. She wrapped her fingers around its swollen head and moved them up and down, agonizingly slowly, then took it inside her mouth.

She worked slowly, licking and sucking, sliding up and down on his cock in a steady rhythm. Gradually she increased the pace, taking more of him inside her mouth, sucking harder.

Don felt the first warning tingle spreading quickly up through his body until he shouted out loud as he exploded in her mouth.

She fell back, grabbed the wine bottle and took a long drink. Don rolled over and sat up. As his eyes refocused, three small, ghastly figures appeared in front of the old shed. Their empty eye sockets were fixed on him and their fleshless fingers pointed at Sally's back. He screamed, and fell back on the grass as the world went dark around him.

From somewhere far away he heard Sally's frightened voice, and he struggled to sit up.

"Lie back," she said. Don kept still for a moment then pushed himself up on to his elbows.

"What happened?" he whispered; then as the awful memory flooded back he sat up abruptly and looked frantically about him.

"You fainted. Don, what is it?"

He clenched his fists and forced himself to calm down. "I'm not sure, Sal. Let's get inside."

Don poured a large whisky, gulped it down, and refilled the glass. Shivering, he put off Sally's questions. He stood for a long time under a hot shower, dried himself, and pulled on a heavy dressing gown. Sitting in the lounge, he told her what he had seen, not mentioning that the figures had been pointing at her, not him.

They talked for a long time, not eating but drinking their way through most of the bottle of whisky. Finally, Sally stood.

"Come on," she said. "We both need some rest. I'll ring in tomorrow and tell Charles you're sick."

Don stood and stretched. "I need some water after all that whisky."

"Bring me some please. I'm off upstairs."

Don went into the kitchen and switched on the light.

The key was lying in the centre of the table.

Don looked at in disbelief, then picked it up and examined it carefully. It was the same key he had thrown in the bin, of that he was sure. Eventually he shrugged and dropped it into the pocket of his dressing gown. He poured two glasses of water and took them upstairs to the bedroom, saying nothing to Sally about the key.

They slept late. Sally called Don's boss to explain that Don had come down with a bad stomach. She took Jack out

122

for his walk mid-morning, and left Don alone in the house.

He took the key from his dressing gown, went downstairs, and sat on the couch. He turned the rusty piece of metal over and over in his hands. After a long while he took the bunch of keys from the hook behind the back door and walked down to the shed.

He removed the padlock and pushed and pulled at the door, but it wouldn't shift.

Reluctantly Don took the rusty key from his pocket, forced it into the lock and twisted it. It turned easily and silently, as if the lock had been freshly oiled. The door swung inwards. Don stepped into the gloomy interior and wrinkled his nose at the musty smell.

There was a noise behind him and he jerked around to see the door swing closed with a thud.

He stood in shock in the darkness. As he was about to move he realized that there was a faint greenish light glowing from above him. As it grew brighter he could see that he was in not in a wooden shed full of tools and boxes, but in a stone cave with a rocky ceiling high above his head. The air in front of him shimmered and for the first time in his life Don experienced absolute terror. The skeletal creature he had seen in the bedroom appeared before him with its bone finger pointed at his heart.

He turned to run, then froze when he saw he was ringed by a dozen of the child-sized, skeletal figures, all with their fingers raised towards him.

Soundless voices filled his brain. "*Be still*!" They screamed. "*We don't want you. We want the child.*"

Don fell to his knees. A frozen fingertip touched his brow, and Don felt a dreadful pain as he fell senseless to the stone floor …

… Don jerked awake as a warm wet tongue rasped across his face.

"Hello, sweetheart," said Sally. "We had a good walk, didn't we Jack?"

Jack leapt up and licked him again, as Don stared blankly at his wife's face.

"What's wrong, love? Were you dreaming again?"

"No. Uh … yes …" Don stuttered. His mind cleared rapidly. "No, it's all right. I must have dropped off."

He jumped to his feet. "How about a cup of tea?"

"Well," said Sally. "If you're so lively, how about sorting out a problem in the kitchen first?"

"What problem?"

"I think there's a leak. Could you have a look?"

Don sighed, and went into the kitchen. Sally followed. He felt fine, but he could remember nothing of what he had done since getting out of bed.

Maybe I'm going nuts, he thought.

"Where's the problem?"

Sally opened the cupboard door under the sink. "In there somewhere. I'll turn the tap on."

Don sank to his knees and peered into the dark cupboard. "I can't hear anything dripping."

"Just a minute."

He heard Sally moving around behind him and he edged forward.

"I don't think …" he began, and banged his head hard as he received a tremendous whack across his backside, followed by a second.

Bemused, he struggled back to his feet.

"Spank me, would you?"

A bowl of icy water was dumped over his head. Sally dropped a big wooden spatula on the floor, dashed out of the kitchen, and fled up the stairs.

Don stood for a moment in shock, and then grinned. He stripped off all his clothes and dropped them in a heap on the kitchen floor. He found a tub of soft ice-cream in the fridge, removed the lid and took it with him to the bedroom.

Sally was lying on the bed, her short skirt up around her thighs. "What do you want, naked stranger?" she purred.

124

He dropped the ice-cream tub on the floor, hopped up on the bed and straddled her waist.

"That was very naughty. I think it deserves a tickling. But first let's get these clothes off."

He stripped her, leaving just her panties, holding her easily in his strong arms. Then he tickled her mercilessly, turning her this way and that and using his fingertips all over her body until she begged him to stop.

Then he settled down above her and ran his cock slowly up and down in the valley between her breasts.

"Spanking? Or should I just tell you how gorgeous you are?"

He leaned down and kissed her. She looped her arms around his neck and closed her eyes as his lips moved to her breasts.

He reached back until his searching hand found the ice cream tub. He scooped up a handful of ice cream, slipped it under the waistband of her panties and dropped the freezing mixture between her legs.

Sally shrieked and jerked as Don grabbed her and pinned her arms to her sides.

"You bastard!"

She wriggled frantically, kicking her legs, but Don held her tight and laughed against her breasts. As her struggles subsided, he released her, reached back down to the tub and dropped another large dollop of ice cream between her breasts. She gasped and shuddered as he smeared it across her nipples.

"Keep still," he whispered. He lowered his head and began to lick, at the same time rubbing the front of her panties, pressing the melting ice cream into her pussy. Her breathing became heavier as he licked and sucked the ice cream from her breasts. He moved down, pulled the panties away and began licking the insides of her thighs, working his way slowly upwards.

She threw her legs wide apart as his tongue parted the

lips of her vagina. He licked with long, steady strokes and she reached a hand to the back of his head to pull him harder against her. His tongue reached her clitoris and moved faster and faster until her body arched upwards and she sank back on the pillows.

Don sat up and took a deep breath. He kissed her and she reached down, twined her fingers round his cock, urging him upwards between her slick thighs until he slid inside her. He moved in and out deliberately, watching her face, refusing to speed up, playing with her, stopping and starting again. Gradually, she began to lose control. Her breath came in shorter and shorter gasps, and she began to moan deep in her throat. Don slowed his pace and she tried to move faster, straining frantically against him.

"Please," she whispered as he stopped moving, his cock buried to the hilt.

Twice more he brought her near to the point of no return, only to stop just before she could come. Her eyes were pleading with him as he started to move again.

"This time," he whispered, and quickened his pace. Her legs rose up around him as she matched his thrusts, until they came together with deep groans of mutual satisfaction.

They lay still for a long time then Don slipped out of her and stood up. "Good stuff, that ice cream." He picked up the tub. "Some more?"

"Don't you dare!"

He laughed and went into the bathroom.

Two days later, Don came home to find his wife in the kitchen.

"I've got something to tell you," she said, eyes gleaming. "I'll get you a drink first."

"Something so bad I'll need a drink?"

Sally laughed. "I hope not," she said, handing him a glass of wine.

"Aren't you having one?"

"No, sweetheart, I'll be leaving the alcohol alone for a

while."

Don stared at her for a minute then a huge grin spread over his face.

"You're pregnant!"

"Yes, sweetheart, confirmed this morning."

"Great! Surely you can have a drop of wine to celebrate?"

"Well, maybe a little drop."

Sally turned and opened the cupboard behind her then snatched her hand back.

"Don!"

He leapt to her side. "What's wrong?"

The key was lying on the shelf, next to the wine glasses.

"You threw it away. I'm sure it wasn't there when I got your glass! I know it wasn't!"

She started to cry and Don put his arm around her.

"Stay here, love. I'll sort this out."

He went back into the kitchen and grabbed the key. As he did so, words echoed in his head and slabs of memory thumped down in his brain.

"We want the child."

"No!" he snarled and felt the key writhe in his hand.

Don strode out to the garage where a spare car battery stood in the corner. He dropped the key into a plastic bucket, unscrewed the cell caps from the battery, and poured acid on it. As the first drops hit it and the surface began to bubble, screaming filled his head and pain flared.

The screaming and the pain went on but he gritted his teeth and sat down heavily on the concrete floor, shaking the bucket to swirl the liquid inside and slowly the noise and the pain died away.

After a long time he stood and looked down. The key was gone. Don took the bucket into the garden, connected the hose, and directed a powerful jet of water into it. Steam rose and the bucket skittered across the grass, spun around and fell against the side of the shed.

Don turned off the hose and examined the shed. The padlock was still there but the old lock had disappeared. Dirty black wood stretched across the whole width of the door. He turned and went back indoors.

Sally was sitting on the couch, stroking Jack.

"It's OK, honey," Don said. "I've really got rid of it this time."

Sally smiled. "I'm sorry," she said. "Was I being silly?"

"No, love." Don rubbed a hand over his eyes. "Forget it! You're going to have our baby! A thought struck him.

"Uh, does that mean we can't …?"

"Of course we can. For months yet." She grinned. "In fact, if you feel like it now …"

Her words were left hanging in the air as Don picked her up and carried her up the stairs.

"Los Hermanos"
by Mark Farley

I love the area I live in. West London is a subtle cacophony of the rich and poor, all kicking their heels in the same places. Myself included, but I am neither rich nor poor.

It's as much of a representation of the many different faces of this city as you will find. Early mornings are my favourite. Even when I am not working, I will get up early for the gym or just to venture out into this melee of society and bask in all of its variety. After all, variety is the key (or is it the spice?) to life. It certainly has been for me since the divorce.

Richard's mother registered relief and glee when he broke the news to his parents over dinner. She never liked me. To his credit, though, he took equal blame as we sat there in our dining room carving into our racks of lamb, despite the majority of affairs originating from my side of the marriage. Not that he didn't have any of his own, he was just more faithful to his one, ongoing mistress (also married herself) than I was with my string of casual male suitors. But I honestly thought that things would pan out in the long run and he would eventually warm to the idea of having children. He didn't, and after five years of asking, we both realised it had become something of a deal breaker in our lives.

I then met David, my younger, and considerably more

eager, lover. He was great and he wanted a family, but I soon realised that he wasn't ready at 23 to do anything apart from clubbing and picking up other girls. In fact, the underlying lack of responsibility and the raging infidelity pretty much brought things to a close. I should have known really. I met him on a website catering for middle-aged women looking to date younger men and he more than boasted that he was working his way through the 30-40 category (in which I come halfway) when we met. So, despite his tremendous abilities as a lover, I came to the conclusion that it was time to move on. So that's what I did.

After a couple of weeks of moping around the flat and watching Sex and the City marathons on Paramount Comedy, I had the urge to have some fun again. Which is when I came across Ruben, who provided me with my recent sexual awakening and gave me the first taste of my new favourite indulgence.

I'd woken that particular morning with a raging libido as well, if I remember correctly. This is strange for me, as normally I'm a 1.30pm-2.30pm kinda girl. Quite precise, I realise and admittedly not ideal for a girl working office hours but, at the weekends, when the shine is cutting through my bedroom curtains, making me feel idle and relaxed, I'm all mine. Plus, there's nothing better than a lunchtime lie-in on a weekend and a pulsating, self-inflicted moment of joy.

I felt naughty and liberated with my new found availability and pondered upon how I could fill the moment with a horny male specimen. Most of my casual encounters had gone silent or were 'spending more time with their wives' so I considered a call to one or two acquaintances. Just guys that had given me their numbers, in a vague hope that I would call. I rummaged through my purse for the business cards and random scraps of paper I had collected, mostly in clubs with my supportive girlfriends who took me out with the premise of being the one who put me on the road to recovery, and tried to recall the people that they belonged to. Nothing.

I screwed them all up in my hand and tossed the creative mound at the small waste basket in the corner, missing it by about two feet.

I discovered my laptop underneath a pile of washing on my bedroom floor, flipped the screen open with the intention of surfing YouPorn.com and momentarily answering the calling in my loins but I got distracted by emails, looking for the new Queen Adreena video, and a slew of Facebook updates to attend to. I'm frustrated about why so many men in Turkey and Israel want to be my friend. As cute as some of them are, I'm in London and they are not. On the flipside, the men in my general vicinity that do try to get through (prompted I suspect by the fact I am single and am in a group called 'Facebook Fuck Buddies') are either ugly, about to draw their pension or wearing a baseball cap and a sneer. The majority of all of the above seem to be in Essex too, which I am not.

I soon realised that the moment and an hour had passed, so I took a shower and headed out for some fresh air. The sun was beating down on the capital and heating all of those post-modernist buildings and Norman Foster constructions, making the city humid, so I opted for my denim shorts and a bikini top with my wedge sandals. I grabbed my big sun hat, shades and a well-loved Jilly Cooper from the bookcase on the way out.

I came to the end of my street and turned onto the Portobello Road. There's a Post Office on the corner, where the infirm and generally useless queue for government handouts every Monday morning. You can set your watches by the agitated looks on their faces as the minutes tick closer and closer to 8 a.m. Before this hour on a weekday, the street is deserted, save for the stink from the night before. The subtle smell of urine catches the back of your throat and mixes there with the warm smell of baked goods from Greggs. When I am down or have my monthly cramps, I nip in for a sausage roll (just for comfort, mind) and bask in the feeling of the delicate pastry melting on my tongue and the crumbs falling onto my chest.

I predictably came across a few of the regular sights. The Marlboro Light-smoking, salt of the earths setting up their fruit and veg stalls. There's that rough-looking blonde girl outside Tesco with the foul mouth. She has her dark roots tied up with a pink scrunchie, attempting valiantly to compete with the 'low, low prices', and pours scornful looks upon the trendy girls in their ballet flats waiting for their boss outside the American Apparel store, looking blank at the prospect of starting their working day. I caught them discussing hedge funds and how their portfolios are doing on the market.

Film producers are perusing scripts outside Progresso, sipping their lattes. They occasionally glance up, hoping to discover the next Kate Beckinsale, or suitable English rose, and blink in bemusement when I glide past with my shocking red hair and exposed tattoos.

When I do go as far as the tube at Notting Hill Gate, I like to stop at the Edwardian butchers to look at the skinned game and award-winning homemade sausages. Occasionally, when I am feeling flushed, I will treat myself to a few, rounded off with my infamous spring onion and Cheddar mashed potato. That day I noticed that they have rare breed beef and salt marsh lamb from Suffolk, whatever that is.

Then there's the imported coffee percolating at the Café Garcia, the heartland of the Spanish community in North Kensington. I could hear the girls yip-yapping in their mother tongue as I approached the sprawling business, which originated from a small grocery store and now also comprises a plush, takeaway emporium. I caught the eye of a rugged Latin in a fitted grey sweater studying a jar of pimentos as I glided past. Our eyes locked for a second.

There's a haunted sense behind the eyes that I recognised as a man's split-moment nonchalance and imagined him kicking himself, especially as I was quick enough to cast a smile in his direction and look down coyly, before I disappeared from view.

About forty feet down the road, I glanced back to see him (sans purchase) step out into the street. A second glance ensured that he was, indeed, following me as I secretly had hoped. He had changed his mind about his groceries, it seemed, and was now in hot pursuit of something tastier. I didn't want to panic him or have him worry that he was being a pest, so I turned and gave him an encouraging smile.

Despite my fear that he would cut and run, I couldn't help but tease him a little. I stopped to look at some shoes in a window and out of the corner of my eye I saw him stop. I smirked inside as he looked as if he didn't know what to do with himself, before innocently carrying on down the road. He was putty in my hands. I darted into The Coffee Plant, my regular stop and, soon enough, I felt his presence behind me as I queued for my organic tea with Soya milk.

"It's all fair trade … and really good," I purred, turning my head slightly in his direction.

"I saw you back there …" he started.

"I noticed." I interrupted, playfully. He offered to pay for my tea as I pulled a note from my wallet. He ordered some Arabica and looked down at my leg. He commented on my tattoo.

"It's new …" I told him, looking down at the Celtic scrawl on my ankle. There was a pause.

"I have lots …" I said, as I sipped and blew the heat from the edge of my cup. We stood awkwardly and he smiled down at me. His well-built frame towered over me, as I wondered if he was the moody, silent type. I also caught myself wondering what he looked like without that sweater on. He looked as though he always appreciated his mother's cooking, like most sons from the Mediterranean do, but then I like a little weight on a guy.

"I'm Siobhan …" I announced, holding out my hand to him. He reciprocated.

"Ruben …"

I asked what he did. Boring, I know. I had to get this off the ground with something though. He told me that he and his brother are architects and told me about the local development they were overseeing.

"I pass that every day. It's noisy." I kidded. Ruben laughed.

He spent an acceptable amount of time talking to my chest (but not too much) and looked as though he was undressing me in his head as I flirted and touched his arm. As he talked about his family in Madrid, he placed his hand on the small of my back a few times. He asked if I was on my way to work and I shook my head innocently, my eyes looking into his.

As we were down to the dregs of our beverages, he asked in his broken English if I wanted to come and see his studio, as it was nearby and has a nice roof terrace. He suggested that we could get a little sun, and I wondered if this translated into Spanish as 'let me fuck you on my sun lounger', but I could be wrong. My mind wandered back to my flat and the comforts of my bed, but the prospect of seeing this guy strip was too tempting.

"Won't your brother be around?" I asked him, as he took hold of my hand.

"No, he's on-site this afternoon …" he announced, guiding me down the street. He walked me five minutes to his building off Ladbroke Grove. The office space they had was fairly small. It was the top floor of a townhouse, which was otherwise converted into flats. They had two rooms, a desk in each, and a bathroom. Filing cabinets appeared overstuffed and there seemed to be more files on top than inside. But then, the whole place could have done with some organising, but there was a distinctly impressive and intricate array of design talent on display. I walked over to an easel to see the evidence for myself. It was definitely technical.

"Is this what you are working on now?" I asked. Ruben appeared, brandishing two bottles of ice tea.

"That is your noisy buildings, yes …" he joked. He pulled aside the curtain and swished open the patio door on to the roof, presenting the terrace with a flourish.

"Nice," I said, with nodding approval. I ditched my hat and my purse and stepped back out into the sun. I put on my shades and lost my top, exposing my boobs to the neighbouring office buildings and, more importantly, Ruben. He seemed to approve. I looked back across to the doorway as I lay back and got myself comfortable on one of the deck chairs.

"Are you going to remove some clothes and join me?"

He pondered on that thought, casually sipping at his drink, before setting it aside and dropping his pants, stepping out of them and kicking off his straw loafers. He peeled off his sweater and tossed it into the shade as he climbed on top of me. I grabbed his bum cheeks and ground each of them in my hands, digging my nails into his hairy flesh as he pushed his mouth onto mine. There was a distinct and musky cigar taste, but his lips were deliciously cool in the heat. He gnawed at each of my breasts like he hadn't eaten lunch as I pulled the hair at the back of his head. I pushed him further down and he took the hint about what I had in mind. He unbuttoned my shorts and left them around my knees, as he flipped me over and pulled my hips back onto his face. I pushed my bum back into him as he lapped away at my scent. I held on to the back of the chair in front of me as he nibbled the base of my spine and thrust three fingers in and out of my hole, making me squelch and squirm.

He got to his feet and stood back to admire the sight

135

before him. Cheeky bugger, he left me panting and in need of so much more. I righted myself and flipped over on to my back. Ruben stood before me, naked and cock in hand. He tore into a condom packet with his teeth and spat the tab to one side. I peeled off the shorts over my ankles and sandals and spread my legs for him. I flicked my button as he pulled the rubber over his fat cock. He wasted no time at all and penetrated me with it, sitting snugly inside me. He eased it in and out of me and buried his tanned face in my neck.

"Let me ride you …" I whispered in his ear. He gallantly leapt to his feet and held out his hand, helping me up. We swapped positions and I sank down onto him. He bounced me up and down for a bit, massaging my boobs and controlling my action on him by grabbing at my hips until I heard a door click and the sound of keys hitting a table.

"Ola Hermano. Que tal?"

I stopped, mid-grind and gasped. I turned to see a man standing in the patio doorway with a handful of maps. He didn't look perturbed or offended and just raised an eyebrow. I did that predictably English thing and tried my hardest to cover my modesty in front of this stranger. I shot my arms around my chest and slid Ruben's cock out of me.

"Oh, don't mind me. You two carry on," he said, disappearing.

I looked down at Ruben, who seemed completely unfazed at his sibling's presence. He shrugged and asked, "Are you OK?"

"Yeah," I said, clocking the whereabouts of my skirt. "Don't you mind him being there?"

He shook his head and announced, "We've seen a lot worse of each other. We're family."

I cupped his wilting cock in my hand and lay next to him.

"In fact," he continued, "we often share …"

"Oh." I realised. "Cool."

He laughed and put an arm around me. We fell silent for a second as I attended to his erection. As soon as I got rid of the rubber, he seemed to respond to the idea of me going down on him.

"Would you like him too?" he moaned with pleasure.

I looked up, with his cock still in my mouth. His eyebrows were raised waiting for an answer. It was something I had always desired, but had never fulfilled. The idea of taking two brothers on was very attractive also. Luis's looks matched his brothers. They were almost identical, if it were not for the height difference. I guess he sensed my curious approval, and enjoyment of the moment, because he called out, "Luis, come … Join us."

Luis appeared at the doorway. He watched me suck his brother's cock and seemed to be looking for my approval.

"Don't be shy, brother," taunted Ruben, lying back and enjoying the attention I was giving him. I stopped and signalled him over. Luis stripped by the door and walked over to the edge of the sun lounger where I was perched. I grabbed Ruben by the arm and made him stand in front of me. Luis quickly joined him and took his place next to his brother. I put a hand on each of their cocks as they stood politely erect for me. I alternated between them for a while, as they wittered away above me in Spanish, about God only knows what.

I shooed Ruben away to get more protection as his brother buried his face in my crotch. He darted his tongue into me and rubbed my clit with his thumb. He sensed my arousal and didn't relent until my hips bucked. I shuddered as I cocked a leg around his neck.

They carried on in their native language as they both moved and positioned me. We moved to a nearby wall which Ruben leant against and had me bend over to suck him off. Luis got behind me and buried his cock into me. They took me at each end for my first spit roast. It felt great. I knew it wouldn't be my last. I had them at my beck and call and they let me playfully guide them all around their flat, having them take me in every possible way, until they gave me their basting and left me with my face covered in their mess.

I staggered back to my flat and soaked my weary, satisfied bones in a hot bath and looked back on my experience with glee and pride. I was certainly back out there now and nothing was going to stop me having fun.

My fling with the Spanish brothers didn't end there either. The Summer is still here, as I write this, and if either Ruben or Luis pass my flat, they call in for a morning wake up call or I meet them both at their office. But only to give my expert opinion on their intricate plans, of course.

The Wardrobe Mistress
by Joe Manx

I'm very close to Aunt Polly, she's my mother's youngest
sister. They're totally different. Polly is outgoing,
vivacious, fun-loving and glamorous, while Mum is a home
bod, likes cooking and quiet nights in. People have often
compared me to my auntie which probably explains why
we're so close. So, it came as a bit of a shock when Polly
suddenly announced she was emigrating. It was a bit of a
whirlwind thing. Her husband died several years ago. She
was devoted to him and I never thought she'd re marry.
Then, after several brief affairs, she'd met an Australian
and, impulsive as ever, had decided to move down under.

'I expect you to visit me,' she said, when I'd expressed
my disappointment, 'we've got e-mail and web cams, it'll
seem as though I'm living next door.'

There was an upside. I'd always loved Aunt Polly's house
and she only lived three miles from us. After a long talk
with my husband, Mathew, we decided to make an offer. To
our delight, Polly accepted and she invited me round to see
if there were any bits of furniture I'd like to keep.

When I visited, Polly answered the door with a bottle of
wine in her hand. She was dressed in a scruffy shirt and
dungarees.

'Hi sweetheart, I've been going through the house,

deciding what to take, what to give away and what to throw away. Come on in, I could do with a break.'

The break lasted about two hours as we polished off one bottle of wine and opened another. We discussed the history of the house, Polly's past relationships and her new Australian boyfriend. I must have sounded a little envious. She turned the conversation to me.

'So, how are you and Mathew getting on?'

'Oh, you know, OK, we've settled into a sort of comfortable domesticity.'

'Sex still good?'

'Polly!'

'Oh come on love, you can tell me, I'll be on the other side of the world soon,' she laughed.

'Well, what can you expect after five years …? It's OK.'

'But it could be a lot better?'

'Yeah, but I suppose, if I'm honest, things have become a little stale lately, a bit predictable. We don't get out much any more, we're both so knackered from work, we just come home and slump in front of the telly.'

Polly smiled. 'Dangerous times love, dangerous times. Do you still love him?'

'Of course I do.'

'The reason I ask is the same thing happened when I was married to your uncle. Without us really noticing, things gradually got very boring. Fortunately, I read a magazine article that described my situation perfectly. It acted as a bit of a wake-up call and I suddenly discovered an unknown erogenous zone that changed everything.'

'And where's that?' I said, intrigued.

'In here,' she said, pointing to her head, 'your brain.'

I laughed.

She smiled.

'If you learn to use your imagination, you can keep your sex life scintillating. Come on, grab the wine, I want to show you something.'

140

We went upstairs and she led me to the end of the landing.

'I call this my wardrobe room,' she said, opening the door of a large bedroom. Along each wall was an enormous Victorian wardrobe. There were racks of clothes and numerous shoes and boots neatly stacked on the floor.

'I didn't know you had so many clothes.'

'Well, you wouldn't have seen me in any of these, sweetheart. These clothes are used entirely for sex. I've never had so much fun and excitement, dressing up and being fucked.'

I must have looked shocked. Polly looked amused.

'I promise you, it's great fun and all men love it … that would include Mathew. Let me show you some of the outfits, I'll let the clothes do the talking.'

Over the next few hours Polly put on various costumes and outfits, demonstrating the part she played, the way she moved and the effect this had on her lovers. I was amazed at the way she transformed both her character and her personal appearance. Burlesque dancer, maid, teacher, secretary, queen, nurse, doctor, she had numerous outfits and accessories. She looked different in each one.

'It's not just about the clothes giving you a different appearance, you take on a different personality as well.'

We're the same size and Polly got me to try on a few outfits. I felt like a different person with each outfit; powerful, subservient, superior, arrogant, meek. It was great fun and exciting.

'I'm going to take my favourite pieces with me but if you're interested I'll leave you the bulk. If it doesn't work out you can send the clothes on to me, but I promise you, sweetheart, once you start, it'll become a lifestyle.'

When we moved I took a week off work and spent several days getting the house up straight. Then, on the third day, needing a bit of a break, I decided to explore the wardrobe room. As I entered the room, I saw, on a little wooden chair, a large, elegantly covered, scrap book. On the front was printed a title:

The Wardrobe Mistress

On top of the book was a letter with my name on it. Inside the letter Polly again described how her hobby had become a passion. 'This book represents years of work, it will open up a whole new world. Use the ideas, build on them – go on, have faith in your imagination!'

I picked up the book and leafed through the pages. It made fascinating reading. There were detailed descriptions of various fantasies. She'd added little notes when a fantasy had been re-played and improved upon. Perhaps she'd used different language or spoken or acted differently. She may have changed or modified the clothing or added accessories. Polly seemed to have perfected a number of roles. Reading about my aunt's adventures was both erotic and arousing. I admired her guts but couldn't see myself dressing up like that, Mathew would just laugh.

Later that day, when Mathew returned home, I was in the bath. Several minutes after his arrival he called out to me, asking if I wanted a drink. A little later, I heard him mounting the stairs and I quickly arranged the foamy bubble bath around me and lay in a seductive pose. He came in with a glass of wine.

'I'm just going to watch the football, love,' he said as handed me the glass. He smiled and walked back out. I lay there for a few minutes, disappointed by the lack of interest in my nakedness. Sod it, I thought, we were definitely in a rut and I needed to do something about it. I dried myself and, glass in hand, wandered through to the wardrobe room. I was nervous but excited.

Leafing through Polly's scrapbook I picked a scenario that wouldn't prove too taxing for a beginner and read her notes. It was a simple game, I just needed the confidence to carry it off. After a little searching I found the 'equestrian' outfit and followed Polly's guidelines.

First, I hung fine, beaded tassels from my nipples. Then I put on

tight beige riding trousers, followed by a tailored, beige riding jacket. I only buttoned the middle of the jacket, which left plenty of cleavage showing. Next, I put on leather riding boots, scraped back my hair and applied lipstick and eye make up. I put on a hard, black, velvet covered riding cap and, with riding crop in hand, inspected the final result in the mirror. The overall result was a rather haughty look. Although a little nervous, I was also feeling aroused. Strangely, the outfit made me feel rather superior.

I wandered downstairs and entered the lounge where Mathew was watching television. I walked slowly, authoritatively, in front of the television and whacked the riding crop against my buttocks. I'd caught his attention.

'Do you like the outfit, it's one of many Aunt Polly left me.'

He looked me up and down.

'You'll need a horse if you're going to take up riding.'

'Oh, I think I've found the animal I want to ride, just need to check it out, make sure I've got a stallion with stamina. Stand up.'

Mathew looked bemused but he also looked interested. He stood up.

'What's all this about then?'

I walked over to him, stood by his side and tapped his bottom with my crop.

'Get undressed I'll need to make a full inspection. Come on, Mathew,' I said, sternly, 'haven't got all day. I want to get some riding done.'

143

The admonishment further aroused Mathew's interest. He began stripping and as he did so, I made appreciative noises. When he was fully undressed his cock was half erect. I walked around him, inspecting his naked body. I ran my crop up and down his back and gently tapped his bottom.

'Mmmm, good flanks, fine legs, good, strong back ...'

Mathew's cock was now fully erect. I ran the tip of the crop slowly up and down its length.

'That's beautiful,' I said. 'I need a strong, smooth, sturdy saddle when I'm riding. The gentle tapping and stroking with the riding crop was having the desired effect. Mathew let out a little gasp. I was now fully immersed in my new role.

'I think this stallion needs to get his oats tonight. I'm going to make sure you're well fed. First of all though, you need a little exercise. Down on all fours!'

Mathew did as he was told. I climbed on his back, took a red, silk scarf from my pocket, leant forward and whispered in his ear.

'Just need to put some reins on you, don't want you getting out of control.'

I placed the middle of the scarf in Mathew's mouth, then sat upright. I held both ends of the scarf in one hand, pulled back his head and gave his bottom a sharp tap with my riding crop.

'Come on now, a nice gentle ride to begin with.'

I was enjoying myself and thoroughly turned on. Mathew carried me slowly around the living room. The riding trousers I was wearing had been ingeniously adjusted. An opening had been made in the crotch of the trousers. Each side of the opening had been lined with a thin sliver of soft fur. I moved my hand down and pushed my fingers through the fur into my pussy. I played with myself for a little while, enjoying the feeling of Mathew's back between my legs, massaging me as he carried me around the room. It was time to spoil myself a little more.

'Whoa, whoa,' I commanded and Mathew halted. I got off him, removing his silk halter, stood over him and raised his chin with my crop.

'That was a nice ride. I think you'll need a little drink now, because soon I'm going to ride you very hard.'

I walked over to a big, soft comfy armchair, sat in it and spread my legs wide, hanging a leg over each side of the armchair. The fur lining between my legs parted revealing my pussy.

'Come on over here, Beauty.'

Mathew let out a mock whinny and I laughed. He came over on all fours and began to pleasure me, licking and nuzzling my pussy.

'You are a thirsty stallion,' I groaned as I felt his tongue and excited breath caressing my pussy. I used my crop to tap his shoulders, giving instructions to speed up or slow down, until he brought me to orgasm. Then I had to put my boots on Mathew's shoulders and push him away as he was still licking voraciously and I wanted cock, I wanted to ride.

'Lie down on your back,' I ordered.

His cock was twitching with excitement. I knelt down astride him, put the silk halter behind his neck and, holding on to the two ends with one hand, I reached back with my other hand and fed his cock into me. We both groaned. I began to move back and forth, holding onto my silk reins with one hand and using the crop on his thigh with the other.

'Just a gentle canter at first,' I moaned. 'Not too fast,' I commanded as Mathew was beginning to buck beneath me, losing control. I was a little harsher with the crop and he slowed down.

'That's better … my, my, this is hard work,' I panted. 'I need to cool down a little.'

I undid my jacket and my tasselled tits stood out proud,

bouncing up and down. I watched Mathew's face and felt his body react with excitement. Again, he began to buck beneath me.

'That's good, faster, faster.'

Mathew took hold of my hips and turned me over. I didn't have the strength to stop him and didn't want to. I was now on my back, legs over his shoulders and he was ferociously pumping into me.

'Come on stallion, that's it, take me to the finish line.'

I could hardly get any words out, I was panting so much. As Mathew pumped into me I gripped a cheek of his bottom with one hand and beat the other cheek with my riding crop, screaming out as I reached orgasm. I felt Mathew shudder and his buttocks tighten as he came. He collapsed on top of me, breathing hard.

'What have you done with my wife?' he laughed, when he'd recovered. 'Enjoy it?'

'That was amazing, darling, thank you.'

I told him all about Aunt Polly's gift. I took him upstairs and showed him the wardrobe's contents. He was plainly excited. Since that day our sex life has been wonderful.

Know what? Mathew said he's going to start his own collection. I'm compiling a list of fantasies for him to think about. I've already written down a number of scenarios.

I've also added to my own wardrobe.

Once, maybe twice a week I surprise my husband. I ring him at work and utter a sentence that he says makes him instantly hard.

Tonight, Mathew ... I am going to be ...

The Waterfall
by Katie Lilly

The first time I saw her she was wearing ugly brown walking sandals, stone-coloured shorts and a tight cotton t-shirt, unsuitable for the narrow, overgrown woodland from which she had just emerged. As she stepped out of the earthy darkness into the shimmering light at the base of the waterfall, she was covered with dirt, sweat and leaves. I imagined her making her way down the slippery path with short, cautious steps, her arms outstretched for balance and to brush away the damp foliage from her face – the tragic heroine of a film.

She was about 35 years old, slender, with long, dark hair clinging to her dirt-speckled face. She walked to the edge of the pool and crouched down. As she scooped up the water and splashed it over her face, droplets fell and, together with the dirt, created a pattern across her chest. Standing up she glanced around before pulling the t-shirt over her head and slipping out of her shorts to reveal a simple black cotton bra and matching thong. As she was slowly wading into the water she stopped, expertly unclipped the bra with one hand and flung it onto the rock where she had left her other clothes. She continued wading into the water, wearing only her sandals and black thong.

The base of the waterfall was peaceful, missed by most of the tourists who walked along the upper path, took a

147

couple of quick snaps and moved on. There was a group of large, grey rocks which helped squeeze the river into a kidney-shaped pool with two eddies of water either side. The whole pool was surrounded by trees and lush, green vegetation. The gushing rush of the water cascading from above filled the air but I found the noise soothing and relaxing.

I was lounging upon one of the rocks directly opposite the waterfall. On my back with my arms above my head, bent at the elbows to form a pillow, I was enjoying the warm sunshine on my naked body. At 42 years old, proud of my physique, I kept fit by walking, cycling and swimming. Enjoying the natural surroundings of the waterfall, I felt a little bubble of frustration at the interruption, nevertheless I watched her with fascination.

With the water lapping around her waist she stopped and began to playfully splash in the water. Scooping up the freshness with both hands she poured it over her head and face, rubbing her arms and small, pale breasts as the water cascaded over her skin. Aroused by her actions I grabbed my cock and, forming an open fist, began to masturbate. I was watching her and, as she waded closer to my position, I slid down the rock to cool my erection in the water. At this moment, her lightly tanned, slender body dipped under the water and emerged with a whoosh a few moments later, about ten feet in front of me.

"Hello there," I said, looking into her big brown eyes and smiling. She was clearly surprised and I can recall her expression as she pushed her hair from her face to return my stare, before casually crossing her arms to shield her breasts from my gaze.

"Hello."

"Beautiful here isn't it?"

"Yes, it is truly amazing."

"I was walking along the top path but couldn't resist taking a peek."

148

She smiled, "Me too."

I can't recall how long we were talking for, but I can remember the shimmering sun moving slowly across the water and, by the time our conversation drew to a close, my rock was in shadow. I found out her name was Heather and she was here alone to recover from a failed relationship in which her partner of almost two years had found someone new to be with. She was talking for most of the time and I was happy to listen. Her voice was light and crisp, her vocabulary betraying a love of literature; the many references to places across America, Europe and Asia, revealing her love of travel.

I was still leaning against the cold, grey stone but was now propped up on my elbows, absorbing the flow of information from her pale, round lips and trying to catch a glimpse of her covered breasts. She shivered a little in the cooling water and I felt my arousal once again. With my lower torso hidden under the water I relaxed and let my cock get hard.

She suddenly dipped under and I lost sight of her. A moment later I felt a rush of undercurrent and warmth around my cock. She flicked her tongue a couple of times around its head and sucked hard to let me know she was there, before surfacing for breath. I eagerly pushed her head back down to show her what I wanted and she was soon back under the water, her tongue working up and down my shaft, her warm juices in contrast to the cool water. This time as she surfaced for air, I lifted my body out of the water and leaned back on the rock, exposing myself for her delight. Placing her arms either side of my thighs she formed a wide, rigid oval with her mouth and took my cock deep inside.

Leaning back I lifted my arse in time to her movements, pushing myself deeper within her. Closing my eyes I listened to the rustle of the trees and the flow of the waterfall intermingled with her soft groaning. The sensations rippling through my cock, travelled up and down my body, causing my temperature to rise and my breath to quicken. I knew if she didn't stop I would soon come, so I reached down and gently tugged at her hair. Lifting her face to mine, my tongue replaced my cock between her pale, round lips as the afternoon sun kissed our bodies.

Heather hadn't planned her encounter with Roger. She was walking along a lightly gravelled path about five feet wide, shown as the easy route on her map, from the mountain village to the waterfall. Hoping for a pleasant afternoon stroll she was only wearing walking sandals, shorts and a t-shirt, not her usual boots and long trousers to protect her legs from insect bites and tics. The path was encased by woodland but the trees were spread thinly and the hot sun was making its mark on her pale, freckled skin. Stopping to drink from a plastic bottle she was carrying, she noticed it was almost empty and hoped she would find a water outlet or spring soon. They weren't marked on the map and she would have missed the last one if it hadn't have been for a 'call of nature' which took her into the woodland.

Heather was enjoying the holiday, the nature, the beauty and the walking. At times she found it difficult to let her mind relax and her thoughts often wandered back to Mike. She would ask herself all the pointless questions that people often did – why wasn't he happy, what does she have that I don't, and would she ever find someone? Overall however, the trip was a resounding success and she did feel a spiritual rejuvenation. The hotel was nice and other guests were friendly although she was a little disappointed that most of them were a good 20 years older than her.

She was pushing back the tangled green mass of ferns to capture a photograph of the waterfall when she spotted a water outlet. Next to the copper pipe was a crude wooden sign with two blue wavy lines and an arrow which was pointing into the undergrowth. Realising it was probably a path, Heather was soon following it in her search of a better photographic vantage point. After half an hour of difficult walking she reached the end of the path and stepped into the sunlight at the base of the waterfall.

She had seen Roger almost as soon as she entered the water. He was about 40 years old with a shaved head covered in a couple of week's worth of dark grey stubble. He had silvery blue eyes, a Roman nose, thin lips and unusually high cheekbones. His broad chest was covered in matching dark grey curls which curved in a snake over his lower abdomen. She couldn't help but admire his tanned physique. As she approached he lowered his torso into the water but the crystal clear pool didn't hide his fully erect cock, suspended a couple of inches under the surface.

The sight of his readiness aroused her and, with arms folded across her chest, Heather was able to discreetly play with her nipples. It was on impulse that she slid under the water, swam towards him and captured his cock as if it was Halloween and she was apple bobbing. As he yanked her from the water and pushed his tongue inside her mouth, she inhaled the heavy scent of his musk and the odour of the damp foliage surrounding them. As she returned his kiss, a fantasy played across her mind, with the handsome stranger, the beautiful waterfall and the newly single woman anxious for adventure.

Parting her legs she straddled him and pushed her pelvis against his cock, the friction of her wet thong rubbing against his taught skin. Detaching from his mouth she leaned back and repositioned her pelvis so his cock was rubbing directly over her clit, stimulating the juices held back by the thin black cotton. Grabbing a breast in each of her hands she massaged them and was flicking at the nipples with her fingernails while he watched with delight. Sensing an orgasm building within her, she increased the pace of her rubbing and, as she closed her eyes and held her breath, she dug her nails deep into the pale pink tips.

151

Heather shuddered and took a deep, noisy breath as a surge of energy radiated out from her body and she climaxed.

Roger immediately pulled at her thong and yanked it aggressively to one side, exposing a cleanly shaved cunt.

"I love shaved pussy," he said, sliding his fingers along the creamy, smooth flesh before exploring inside. Taking the weight on her legs, Heather tilted her pelvis to allow him deeper inside. She was filled with her own juice and ready for more as she reached down and pulled his hand away, grabbing his cock and sliding it inside.

"Fuck me," she said, smiling.

Roger grabbed her arse and, lifting his pelvis, slid her flesh up and down his shaft, controlling the pace at a slow glide. Heather let him guide her movements at first, but, as her excitement built and the urge for more of his hardness to fill her became stronger, she pushed harder, deeper and increased the pace.

"Slow down or I'll come."

She obeyed his command and eased back a little to give him a lighter ride, but Roger was unable to contain himself any longer. She felt his body shudder and, as he gasped for air, his cock exploded, shooting its hot, creamy satisfaction deep inside. As quick as a rocket Heather lifted off and, with his semi-hardness nestled under her nude pussy, she let out a torrent of hot, steamy liquid and covered him with her piss. Leaning forward she placed her lips on his and kissed him until she had released every drop of her golden delight and then she slid into the water.

As the sun was making its late afternoon journey across the sky, Heather was playfully splashing in the water. I was still leaning against the cold, grey stone but was now propped up on my elbows, trying to digest the afternoon's activities. She was shivering in the cooling water, which was no longer fed by the sun's warmth.

"It's getting cold," I said.

"Yes, I need to get out of the water."

"Good idea," I replied as she turned and began making her way through the grey shadows back towards her side of the pool and her waiting clothes. "But I'm this way and my clothes are this side."

She was slipping away, moving with a purpose towards the edge of the pool and if I didn't act quickly I knew I would lose her. "I think the path back up to the top is less steep on my side."

With the water lapping below her knees she hesitated and, turning to face me, looked at the path from which I had descended before turning to face the steep incline in front of her. Glancing back once again she spoke softly to the mountain air above my head.

"I guess I could wade over with my clothes."

I waited anxiously in the middle of the pool as she picked up her clothes, map, water bottle and camera, before slowly wading back into the water, her things held tightly against her upper chest. I watched her advancing towards me, her lightly tanned body beautiful in the fading light. We met once again and I led the way towards the opposite side of the pool. Illuminated by the last of the sunlight we followed its warm, guiding rays to the shoreline.

I exited the water first and, keeping my back towards her, reached my clothes in five large, solid strides across the pebbled shore. I struggled to pull the thick, navy denim jeans over my wet legs, harnessing my re-awakening energy behind the steel zip. I pulled my white t-shirt over my head and was slipping into my sandals as I turned to check on Heather, who stood about eight feet behind me. Fully clothed, she was brushing at the front of her t-shirt, attempting to remove the dirt stains she had picked up earlier.

"You look fine," I said, smiling and moving towards her.

"I thought it might come off now that it's dry."

"I can hardly tell it's dirty, I'm sure no one will notice."

153

"Shall we make a start, which way is the path?"

"This way, follow me."

We strode out towards the line of lush green vegetation which soon opened up to reveal a lightly gravelled path that would take us back to the top of the waterfall. The path was damp but firm as it meandered through the woodland in a series of hairpin bends, designed to keep the incline to a minimum. Keeping my pace slow and my strides measured, Heather was easily able to keep up and, as the path widened out, she took the lead, walking a few metres ahead.

I was taking in the beauty of the woodland in the fading light as we walked in silence, heading towards the village, but I was easily distracted by Heather. I watched her long, dark hair blowing in the gentle breeze, her marching arms helping her keep up a steady pace, and those long slender legs. I was staring at the unflatteringly baggy stone-coloured shorts which covered her peach-shaped arse and wondered if the wet thong had been removed. Quickening my pace I caught up to Heather in two large strides and pushed my hands up the back of her thighs and underneath the baggy fabric, squeezing her arse. The thong was absent.

I removed my hands and hugged her around the waist, pulling her towards me. Holding her close we walked together in mechanical fashion and I steered us off the path, stopping in front of a large tree. Quickly, I unzipped her shorts and thrust both hands inside the fabric, rubbing the smooth, hairless pussy as my erection grew inside my jeans. I pushed my fingers into her crevices, already wet with anticipation and gently released my warm breath into her ear. Her soft flesh yielded to my touch as, using both hands, I tried to reach deep inside.

"Let's take them off," I said already pulling the shorts over her legs. She obligingly stepped out of them and, free of their restriction, spread her legs wide learning forward and bracing her elbows on the tree trunk.

"Fuck me," she said in a whisper. "You know I want

you."

With my left hand I reached up under her t-shirt and bra while my right hand returned to her delicate smooth folds of flesh. In synchronised perfection I flicked, pinched and massaged her nipple and her clit, determined to bring her pleasure. Ignoring the pain of my bulging cock rubbing inside the coarse denim, I was working in a steady rhythm, until her groans told me it was almost time.

Fumbling a little with the zip of my jeans, I released my cock, already shining with pre ejaculate, and slipped it easily up inside her cunt. Placing my hands on her hips I pulled her towards me as I began to fuck her, but she sharply pulled away and I slipped out of her. Reaching back with her hand, she grabbed my cock and re-positioned it over her arse hole. "I want you to fuck me here," she said.

Tentatively I pushed a couple of inches of my cock inside her taught little hole, too nervous to slide very far. Heather responded by pushing closer to me and, grabbing my arse with her hand, pulled me deeper inside. Guiding my body she soon had the whole length of my cock deep in her wonderful flesh.

"Spank me," she instructed and I tapped her arse cheek with my palm, gently at first and then more forcefully in response to her disapproval of my efforts. With every spank I was turning her peachy skin to rosy red.

"Now, fuck me up the arse, hard and strong."

Taking a deep breath and holding her hips I began to thrust, slowly at first but I was soon gathering momentum. The sensation was amazing as the flesh pinched my cock and I felt the resistance of her tight anal muscles. I was excited and a little disgusted at the same time, as I pounded her delicate frame with all my strength. Heather, with her arms now outstretched and supported by the tree was pushing back strongly onto my cock and groaning loudly. I was hardly aware when she reached down and began stroking her clit. With expert precision she circled this pink peak and brought herself to fulfilment.

Heather shouted out as she climaxed and a huge suction wave engulfed my cock, stopping it in mid thrust. A few seconds later I resumed fucking her, my confidence increasing, each slide opening her gorge a little more to accommodate my girth a little easier. I closed my eyes and let the light flicker inside my eyelids, slowing to relish the final few thrusts before forcing my salty essence into her innermost recess. Groaning with pleasure, I let her arse devour every last drop before withdrawing across her rosy cheeks. Realising that I was fully relaxed I took a step back and, taking my spent cock in hand, I allowed the hot, golden liquid to flow. Pouring it over her arse I let it run down those slender thighs and over her sensible brown walking sandals. The silence was displaced by the spraying hiss of my piss and my sigh of satisfaction as a pungent odour filled the air. It was a day I would never forget.

The afternoon sun is almost lost, casting its eerie glow over the garden as it waves goodnight and the tinkling ripple of the waterfall competes for attention with the evening birdsong. I am relaxing in my favourite spot, leaning back in the wooden reclining chair, next to a small, round table, facing towards our garden pond. I close the notebook which I am holding and put it down on the table, resting my blunt pencil on the bright blue cover. I am proud of my afternoon's work and let a smile escape.

I hear her approaching along the white gravel hairpins, long before I see her. As she stands in front of me, her long dark hair waves gently in the breeze and I admire her body.

"Dinner's ready," she says with a smile.

"I've just finished."

"Is it good?"

"Yes, I'm very pleased with how it turned out."

I get out of the chair and walk across the lawn, stopping in front of her. Reaching up, I cup her face and caress her

156

round, pale lips with my thumb, before leaning forward to kiss her. With my other hand I gently cup her breast and skim over the thin, yellow cotton before coming to rest protectively over her swollen abdomen.

"I love you Heather," I whisper.

"Fuck me," she says with her smile and reaches out for my cock.

Something Wicked This Way Comes
by Jim Baker

SETH RAN HIS EYES slowly back and forth across the door, studying its peeling paint and green corroded brass handle. Bees buzzed in his brain. His fingers tightened on the key he was clutching in his hand, and blood ran down his palm as it dug into the flesh. He felt eyes upon him, and turned. A curtain flickered in the window of the house next door, and he glimpsed a woman's face. He raised his hand to his face, licked the blood from his fingers, and blew a mocking kiss from crimson lips. He lifted a bony finger and beckoned her, grinning mirthlessly as the curtain closed abruptly. He turned and thrust the key into the lock.

Jane shuddered as she watched him. She felt icy cold, even though the room was filled with sunlight. The gaunt figure had seemed to be surrounded by a cloak of dirt, cold, and misery. Grime clung to him like iron filings to a magnet. Greasy stubble blackened his chin. Long, matted dark hair hung to his shoulders, and his fingernails were filthy black arcs. She squeezed her eyes closed. When she opened them he was still there, staring at the town house next door. She flinched as he swung around and blew her a kiss from bloody lips framed in a white, skeletal face. A long finger beckoned and she flung the curtain down and jumped back.

Seth pushed open the door and stepped inside. The house

was chill and dark. He sniffed the damp air, walked down the hallway, and opened a door. As his eyes grew accustomed to the gloom he saw the outline of a window, shielded by thick curtains. He strode forward and yanked them open, then threw his hands to cover his eyes as bright sunlight bit into the room. Slowly he uncovered his eyes and stood still, his body shimmering.

The shadows formed, as they always did, black and tiny. They began their dance in the corners of the room, slowly growing bigger and darker. They moved toward him. The sunlight retreated as they got larger. Standing motionless, he waited for them to envelop him. He knew she would come. He was content to wait for her, in their warm darkness.

"For Christ's sake, Jane, stop gazing out of the window. I've had a lousy day at work, and the last thing I need is you ranting on about some lunatic next door!"

Paul heaved himself up from the armchair, and stomped to the bar.

"I might as well get myself a drink. You seem to be well ahead already."

He poured himself a whisky and looked over at his wife, who was still gazing out of the window, a gin and tonic in her hand.

She turned and smiled weakly.

"I'm sorry, Paul," she said, "you didn't see him. He was filthy and horrible. Then there was the blood and everything. And he knew I was there. He beckoned me ..."

"You didn't go near him, did you?"

Paul glared his wife at his wife as she hesitated.

"No ... no, of course not!"

But something was nudging the edge of her consciousness, a memory of black shadows and of cold and dirt – of intense delight ...

Seth was standing in the centre of the room when she

entered. He turned to look at her with glittering eyes and her body shuddered with fear, but her feet led her to him. She could smell death on him, mixed with a promise of unbelievable pleasure.

She walked over to his indistinct form, entered the shadows that surrounded him and at once felt warm and unafraid.

He wound one hand into her hair and yanked her head back, holding it in a merciless grip while he kissed her. His lips were icy and hard, his breath was fetid, and his eyes glittered green. His tongue probed for hers and he sucked it deep into his mouth. He stripped away her blouse and her bra and mashed her breasts with a calloused hand. He twisted and pinched her nipples between a grimy finger and thumb. Jane felt jabs of pain that dissolved into bursts of pleasure, rushing up to her brain and down ... down to her hot, wet, throbbing cunt. She felt she was screaming, but nothing broke the silence in the pit of shadows that danced ever higher around them.

He dropped his head and feasted on her breasts, sucking on her engorged nipples while his hand worked on the fastenings of her jeans. She helped him, kicking them away, frantic to divest herself of any clothing.

He pulled her down on to the cold floorboards and ripped her panties away. She opened her legs wide and he knelt between them, pushing her thighs further apart with his hands. His head dropped down; she felt his breath on her cunt and then his lips and tongue, licking and sucking the hot flesh. His tongue slid inside her, long and hard and he fucked her with it as her body writhed on the cold floor. Then he took her clitoris between his lips and Jane screamed silently as he sucked mercilessly and rasped his tongue across the swollen button. She twisted her nipples frantically between her fingers; his tongue worked faster and faster as she raced towards her climax. The orgasm was nothing like she had ever known. There was a roaring

*in her ears and bright coloured lights flashed behind her
eyelids as she came in a huge racking burst of pleasure. She
felt hot liquid squirting from her cunt and heard the
slurping sounds from below as Seth gulped it down ...*

"Hello, hello, world to Jane!"

She blinked hard and stared across the room at Paul, who
was looking at her worriedly.

"Sorry, darling, what did you say? I must have been
daydreaming."

"I thought you'd gone off into outer space." Paul still
looked concerned. "What on earth were you thinking
about?"

Jane struggled to remember but whatever it was
remained stubbornly just below the surface of her memory
and she shook her head.

"I don't know."

She rubbed the hot, wet flesh of her thighs together and
gave a little shiver of pleasure.

*Seth stood in the shadows, for the moment replete. The
juices of the woman would not sustain him for long. But the
next time she would bring seed from her man. After that, he
would need the man himself.*

He smiled.

Jane woke early. She had slept badly, disturbed by dreams
of shadows in a dark room of a cold house. There was
something she had to do, but couldn't remember what. As
she lay, struggling with her memory, Paul rolled against
her. The warm touch of his body acted like the turning of a
switch. A craving filled her.

She sat up and hauled the bedcovers away, kicking them
off the bed with her feet. Paul woke and looked blearily at
her as she pulled her nightdress over her head and threw it
aside.

"Janey, what the hell …"

He got no further. She straddled his knees and wrapped a hand around his semi-erect cock.

"Janey …"

"Hush, baby. Lie still."

He fell back on to the sheets as she played with his cock, jacking it slowly between her fingers. It grew hard and she brought her other hand up to it and tickled the sensitive skin under the head with her fingernails, then tickled his balls until Paul groaned with a mixture of pleasure and frustration.

She moved up the bed and kissed him, her fingers still working.

"Come on, sweetheart. Put this big hard cock right up inside me and fuck me stupid." She rolled on to her back and pulled him with her so he fell between her open thighs. Paul was still half groggy from sleep, but her excitement transmitted itself to him and the bedsprings twanged as he thrust furiously into her.

Seth stood on the other side of the bedroom wall listening to the sounds of lovemaking. He smiled and the shadows danced high as Paul's long drawn-out gasp announced his climax. Now the woman would have something more to bring him.

Jane sat at the kitchen table, staring into her empty coffee cup. Paul had gone to work, sated and confused by Jane's frantic desire for sex.

He had come very quickly the first time, and fallen back on the sheets, desperate to sleep, but Jane had demanded more.

She had worked on him with fingers and lips until he was hard again. Then she straddled him, rode him to a second orgasm, and milked every last drop of sperm from him while he moaned with pleasure.

But she had felt nothing. No ecstatic waves, no orgasm.

Nothing.

She stood and walked out of the house to return to the source of pleasure that still plagued the edge of her memory.

A week went by.

The summer evening was drawing to a close and the sunlight was fading from where they sat in the patio garden.

"He's watching us again."

Jane stared at her husband.

"He's at the bedroom window. Watching us."

Paul sighed inwardly and took a long drink from his glass of wine.

"Jane, it's his window. We can't stop him looking out of it."

"Don't patronize me! I wasn't going to say, but since you seem to think Svengali next door can do no wrong, let me tell you he had a go at me yesterday!"

"Had a go at you?"

Paul rose and put his hand on his wife's shoulder.

"What happened?"

"He came out when I was in the front garden. He stared at me and started this mumbling, like a chant. Then he screamed something horrible about me."

"What do you mean, about you?"

"He called me a cunt and a whore!"

She started to cry.

Paul stood up.

"Right. I'll sort the bastard out!"

He marched into the house and fuelled his indignation with a large glass of whisky.

Seth moved away from the window as the sun died. The woman had reacted as expected. Salvation was on its way.

Paul raised a hand to hammer on the door. It swung open in welcome, and dark silence beckoned. Mindlessly, he stepped over the threshold, climbed the stairs, and pushed open the door at the top.

Seth turned to face him, and held out his hand to guide him into the shadows. He stroked Paul's hair and his face with his dirty hands. His thin lips smiled mirthlessly and his eyes glittered in anticipation.

Paul stood motionless as Seth undressed him slowly, dropping each garment on the wooden floor. He caressed Paul's stomach and thighs with his fingertips, and then brought his calloused palms together to clasp his cock, which stood upright, rigid, swollen, and red.

He rolled the column of flesh in his palms as he kissed Paul lightly on the lips, and then dropped to his knees in front of him. Paul shuddered as Seth took the head of his cock between his lips and began to suck.

The shadows darkened and quivered, as Seth took more and more of the cock into his mouth. He sucked harder and harder, his fingers pumping at the shaft, until the climax hit Paul and he groaned as he shot burst after burst of hot seed into Seth's mouth.

The shadows vibrated crazily and slowed as Seth sucked the last drops. He stood, kissed Paul again on the lips and played gently with his soft cock, which began to grow hard once more. The shadows grew tall and enveloped the pair in darkness.

"You were a long time. What did he say?"

Paul looked blurrily at his wife.

"Nothing. He wasn't there."

"But … where have you been, then?"

Paul shook his head. "I don't know."

Jane stared silently at him.

Tiny black shadows began to dance in the corners of the room.

When We Were Two
by Sommer Marsden

"This is the story of how we begin to remember," Steve said and locked the front door.

"What are you talking about?"

My mother drove off. She beeped three times and I saw a flock of hands waving from the car windows. Her exhaust pipe plumed in the cold air as she took my children for four long days.

"How we begin to remember what it is to be Steve and Laurie."

I folded the throws scattered around the living room. I fluffed pillows, glanced back out the window, looked for something to keep me busy. With a house full of kids: fourteen, twelve, nine, and seven, it's never hard to be busy. Now it was quiet. Silent. Eerie. I wanted to whip out my cell phone and call my mother. I wanted to demand my busy, chaotic house back.

Stephen read my face. He took my hands and kissed me. It took the edge off the anxiety but not entirely. "What do we do?" I asked. And sadly, it was a sincere question.

"Relax and enjoy it. I know it's odd. It seems entirely new. Like we have never, ever been alone before," he laughed. "But close your eyes and think way back. Way back when. Once upon a time, we were two. Not mom and dad. Steve and Laurie."

I closed my eyes and found it hard to breathe. My ears kept straining for the sounds of siblings fighting or something being broken. The sounds of a shower running or a too loud stereo or someone on the phone demanding that the caller, *"Shut up ... Noooo ... oh, shut up!"*

"That was a really long time ago. I don't think my memory goes back that far," I laughed. But it was a nervous, high laugh. A dead giveaway that I was telling the truth. Spitting out a fact disguised as humour. "I can't remember what it was like before they filled the house up with noise and kids and chaos."

And it was true.

"I seem to recall that you liked this," my husband said and dropped to his knees. His jeans made a whispery sound on the hardwood floor and he peeled my leggings down like he was unwrapping a present. My black Danskin leggings that were so much easier to put on than a fancy outfit. Even faster than jeans when it came to a hectic schedule.

Instinct took over. Anyone could walk in. I pressed my thighs together and twisted away from his face. Contorted in the opposite direction despite the fact that his face being near me, his breath on my plain cotton panties, made me wet between the legs. Made my heart speed up from something besides anxiety.

Steve put his hands on my hips. Hips that has supported four pregnancies and were definitely wider than when we started our marital adventure. "Shh now, Laurie. No one here but us. Now just let me. Come on, let me."

I did. I let him peel down my panties in the bright sunny living room. Let him touch his tongue to my clit. I let him slide his fingers into me and probe against those sweet wet spots that made me clutch at his big shoulders. I let out a little cry as he slid his fingers free of me. When he latched his lips over my clit and started to lick more of those lazy circles, I felt tears leak from the corners of my eyes. It felt so good to let go. He felt good. I let my thighs fall open in

166

invitation. He could finish that or he could slide into me. I was happy either way.

How quickly I had changed my mind. It was starting to come back to me in bits and pieces. Like a dream that you only recall hours later when you sit quietly with a cup of coffee.

"Not yet," he said and continued his languid tour of my cunt. "We used to take our time. Remember?"

"Not always." More of it came flooding back to me. The time when we were two. Sometimes we were hurried. In a frenzy of clothes and hormones and I could barely breathe until he slipped his cock inside of me and fucked me. "Sometimes we were like crazed animals," I laughed. This laugh was lower. More sultry. Not nervous at all.

Stephen kissed the jut of my hip bones and the swell of my belly. Little silver stretch marks tattooed that skin. I hated them for the most part, but when he kissed them they seemed important. Meaningful. He drew his tongue over the surge of flesh that were my hips, the little landslide of freckles that I loathed and he loved. He kissed my ribcage below my breasts. He did all of this slowly. As if we had all the time in the world. And we did, or so it seemed.

His tongue wrapped the very tip of my nipple and an invisible cord of pleasure inside of me was tugged. I felt the warm sensation of want shoot from my nipple to my pussy. I spread my legs wide and wormed my hand between us to find his erection. He skittered away from me, "Not yet, not yet," he scolded.

"You are stubborn."

"I am remembering. I am recapturing the time long ago. Now we constantly wait for the knock on the door or the sick kid or the fight that interrupts. Or we have to wait until the middle of the night and then we're both tired. This is nice right now. This is what it used to be for us. This is what we are going to make it again. Starting now. A new leaf."

167

His mouth came down on me again. Hot and wet and very welcome. I arched back, into his embrace. Calming myself. There was time to be frenzied later. Four days. Four days of … whatever we wanted.

A little breathless at the thought, I pushed him away. He argued but then his eyes found mine and he let me go. His curiosity won over his desire to keep his mouth on me. "I seem to remember," I said, climbing slowly to my feet. I stifled a small groan. The wooden floor was unforgiving and I was no longer twenty, "that you liked when I danced for you."

A ribbon of unease unrolled in my belly. Could I pull this off at forty-something? Could I be the sexy dancing siren? He smiled up at me. His face a mess of dark stubble peppered with grey. More lines around his big blue eyes. His jaw line a bit softer than it was back in the day. Gorgeous. He smiled wider and I had my answer. I could.

I touched my toe to the stereo button and our station came on. Something classic, something slow. I moved to the music as best I could. Focused on his eyes on me. Of how his mouth had felt on my skin. I closed my eyes and let that feeling take over my motions. I let my hands peel off my plain mom bra that Stephen had bunched down under my breasts. I tossed it over my shoulder with attitude, as if it were the most expensive black lace lingerie.

My husband growled low in his throat and I forgot my self-doubt.

"There she is," he said and reached up between my legs to touch me.

I let my head fall back. Let his touch and the music move me. Push me and pull me. "Who?"

"The Laurie I fell in love with. She's always been here but I haven't seen her so clearly for a long time."

Me either, I wanted to say. I didn't. I swallowed the words and focused on how I felt.

"You are more beautiful now than ever."

"After four babies?" I laughed, swaying my more generous hips. I squeezed my breasts and swayed to the music.

"Absolutely. More beautiful after every one. Most beautiful now," he said. Then he was on his knees again, his head pressed against my lower belly as I moved. I slid down to join him, pushing him back.

"If memory serves, this is something else you like," I said and kissed my way over his chest. I trailed my tongue down his belly and the muscles fluttered just under his skin. His breath caught, a sound that never fails to make me wet, to turn me on. The sound of stealing a man's breath is amazing. The fact that I still could, even more so. I smiled and captured his cock in my mouth, sliding the length into my throat. I had memorized his taste and texture long ago but this time seemed new. New flesh. New meaning.

His hands went into my hair. Immediately and forcefully. I sucked him harder. I worked my tongue over every ridge and dip and swell until I felt light-headed.

"Come on. Now, Laurie. We've been patient enough," he laughed and I laughed with him.

"And we have the rest of today and then three whole days after," I agreed.

"Yes, yes, we can have dinner and go for an encore," he said and tugged my hand. Pulling me up to him.

I straddled his hips and ever so slowly lowered myself onto him. I stared him right in the eye. My husband. My friend. My gaze never left his and that itself brought a huge power with it. A renewed connection.

"Baby," he said. Nothing more. Just the one word.

I came. My body squeezing around him as he lost his patient rhythm and thrust up under me, his hips beating an erratic tattoo against the scuffed but polished hardwood floor.

"Baby," I said back and watched his face when he came. I had seen it more times than I could count but it seemed like the first.

When I kissed him and he pinched my nipple, I laughed. I felt grateful. Grateful for our family and what we had built, but grateful that for just a few days, we could be two again. To be adventurous again. To have sex on the floor in the sunshine.

"Do you remember?" he asked.

"I do."

Who's Been Wearing Aunt Clarissa's Panties?
by Jeremy Edwards

If I recall correctly, it was raining on the day I helped Megan sort through all the junk in her attic. Of course, it may just be that since the atmosphere up there felt so warm and snug, my memory has embellished the cosy scene with a proverbial rainy-day backdrop. Whatever the weather, I remember feeling that we were sort of like kids, taking advantage of a day off from school to mess around gleefully indoors.

In reality, Megan and I were in our late twenties. At that point we'd been together for nearly a year, but I don't think I'd ever been in her attic before. She had learned, however, that I had a talent for organising things – especially other people's things. And when I'd volunteered to take part in the Great Attic Junk Sort of 1998, she had literally leapt at the offer, popping up from her snack at the kitchen counter and smothering me in peppermint-ice-cream kisses.

So there we were, vacuuming up vintage dust bunnies; dividing toys into the "sentimental value" pile, the "yard sale" pile, and the "broken" pile; and talking at length about the highlights of Megan's childhood. What I had anticipated being a chore had actually proved to be one of the most enjoyable, comfortable times we'd ever shared, a taste of what it would be like to live together and last together.

I soon observed that Megan was particularly interested in a trunk of old clothing. As she explained, she fondly remembered playing dress-up with her sister Katie, out of this very trunk, in this very attic. You see, when her parents moved down to Florida, Megan had returned from the big city to purchase the house she grew up in. This was both strange and wonderful to me. Personally, I couldn't imagine wanting to live out my adult life in my childhood home – pleasant though my family house, and my experiences in it, had always been. Yet Megan felt she belonged in her parents' former house. And knowing this made me recognize the chummy old three-story as a sacred, privileged place in which to spend time with her, grow with her, and deepen in my love for her. In a way I couldn't quite pinpoint, Megan seemed to really come to life here. This was where her personality seemed to reach its fullest expression, her joys attain their richest development, her wisdom and emotions gain their greatest depth. I could swear that she even had better orgasms here than over at my place.

She was about a third of the way through sorting and folding the hodgepodge of clothes in the trunk. Suddenly she spoke with an intriguing catch in her voice, a noticeably different tone from that of the casual chitchat we'd been engaged in. "Now *these* I need," was what she said.

I looked up. In her hands was a pair of retro panties, by far the most beautiful thing I'd seen today in Megan's attic – apart from Megan herself.

Based on what I'd absorbed from old *Playboys* (many of which were in *my* parents' attic), they looked like they must have been from the 1950s or 1960s. They were full-cut, black nylon panties – those high-waisted, generous undies from before bikini cuts took over. They had straight hems at the leg openings, where they would modestly clasp a lady's upper thighs. And what made this pair special was that almost every inch was covered in lace ruffles, like you

172

might find on the front of a tacky tuxedo shirt from the 1980s. But this was a lot better than a tuxedo shirt, I assure you.

"Wow!" I exclaimed. "What are *those*?"

"Aunt Clarissa's panties," Megan answered thoughtfully. She clutched the garment to her chest.

"Ah," I replied. I waited the obligatory three seconds that we natural comedians instinctively feel. Then I said, "Who is Aunt Clarissa?"

She placed the panties back in the trunk – tenderly, I noticed. "Clarissa is my mom's younger sister. When we were little, she lived in New York, and so we got to see her pretty frequently. Katie and I thought she was so neat! She's always been a real free spirit – an independent woman. I mostly remember her from the late 70s, when she would show up and take us waterskiing, or teach us disco steps. And when Clarrie was younger, according to Mom, she was quite the bohemian. She lived in London for a while, hung out with artists, wrote film reviews, partied a lot, and did her own thing. That would have been back in the 60s, before I was born. I've seen pictures of her at that age, and she was pretty hot. There's even a family rumour that Aunt Clarissa did some nude modelling for a high-class photographer. Unfortunately, I've never been able to track down any of *those* pictures – and don't think I haven't tried!"

We laughed at the image of Megan assiduously attempting to dig up nude pictures of her beloved aunt.

"Mom loved her life here – Dad, the family, the house, yours truly and kid sister Katie – but I think she admired Aunt Clarissa for going out into the world in the way she did. One thing's for sure: Katie and I idolized her. Sadly for us, Aunt Clarrie eventually moved out to the West Coast, and since then I've hardly ever seen her. I adore her letters, though."

"She sounds really cool," I said, fatuously but sincerely.

173

"And any hero of yours is a hero of mine. Now – uh – about the panties …"

Megan smiled, enjoying as she always did the erotic tilt to my train of thought. "Yes, the panties." She came and sat on the floor with me.

"A few months ago, I was rummaging through the clothes in this trunk. At that stage, I wasn't serious about organising things. To tell you the truth, I was probably procrastinating, when I had some type of deadline looming. Anyway, I came across these vintage panties – or 'fancy pants,' as they're called."

I burst out laughing. "Fancy pants?"

She chuckled with me. "Hey, that's what they're called. I looked it up."

"But that's the title of a Bob Hope movie."

Megan shrugged. "They're also known as 'sissy pants', or 'rhumba panties', if you prefer."

"Can't I just call them 'Aunt Clarissa's panties'?"

"Works for me."

"Okay. But then … how do we know they're Clarissa's?"

"Mom told me. She was here for a visit shortly after I'd discovered them, and I innocently asked her if they were *hers*. It was hilarious, Arthur! Mom raised an eyebrow, in that way she does, and said 'Those were Clarissa's.' So I asked if we should send them to Aunt Clarrie in California, but Mom kind of cleared her throat and hinted that they might not quite fit anymore. I was going to donate them, and then …"

Here was where I became even more interested. "And then … what?"

"And then … I realized I liked them. I realized I liked them a lot. They were practically good as new, and it was as if they were just waiting for somebody to wear them again. After Mom went home, I came up here and held the panties in my hands. I thought about Aunt Clarissa wearing them, and how sexy she must have looked. And felt."

I was starting to feel a pleasant tension in my groin. "I bet you were tempted to try them on."

Megan's eyes flickered mischievously. "More than tempted." Her face lit up even further as she reminisced. "Arthur, they felt so – well, I guess 'erotic' is the word. They hugged all my – you know – womanly parts very sensuously. I stood looking at myself in the mirror, in a way I never had before. Looking and … touching myself." She licked her lips.

I was mesmerized, and my own erotic parts were buzzing with excitement as I visualized what she had described.

Megan proceeded with her explanation. "When I was around Clarrie in my childhood, I was too young to understand sexuality. I just thought she was cool, and smart, and funny. She used to tell us riddles and listen to rock radio in the car with us. But looking back now, I have a strong sense of how sexual she was – still is, I'm sure, because that never goes away, even if you can't fit into your sissy pants any more."

At that moment, I could look into our future and see Megan as a sixty-year-old, sexy as ever. And I welcomed the thought of waking up naked in bed with her at that – or any – age.

Twenty-nine-year-old Megan was still speaking. "I think when I became a grown woman, my memories of Clarrie shaped themselves into a kind of unconscious sexual role model – my ideal of an attractive, self-actualized, sexually-alive female."

"Well, if that's what you were going for, you've certainly lived up to your ideals!" I proclaimed. Megan was certainly *my* ideal of womanhood.

She smiled appreciatively. "Thank you, sweetheart. So the panties … the panties, I suppose, really made me connect with what I thought was sexy about someone like

Aunt Clarissa, and with my own sexuality, too."

This was fascinating. And it made me think about how much *I* wanted to connect, at that instant, with Megan's sexuality – in the most literal, physical manner.

"I was tremendously impressed by how special these panties made me feel," she continued. "I've probably worn them half a dozen times since then."

"All by yourself?" I rasped.

"Yes," she replied. She paused a second, then spoke again. "Until now, that is." And she stood, picked up Aunt Clarissa's panties, and began to walk down the stairs. Right before she descended out of sight, she turned and blew me a kiss.

Since I perceived an intermission in the developing drama, I took the opportunity to wash up. When I came out of the second-floor bathroom, I saw a light through the open door of the master bedroom. I walked in.

"I'll be out in a second!" Megan called from the walk-in closet, after she'd evidently heard me clomping around her room. I stripped down to my briefs – it seemed the thing to do – and then I sat on the bed to wait for her. I stroked the quilted texture of the comforter as I imagined what Megan would look like in Aunt Clarissa's panties.

I did not have to imagine for long.

She was wearing the panties, and only the panties. Looking her over, I saw soft brown hair, luscious eyes with long, lazy lashes, milky shoulders, quiet, bare little breasts, and a dream of a petite, convex tummy. And I saw Aunt Clarissa's panties – now so effectively occupied.

Thank goodness these panties had not gone legging off to California. Though Megan always looked lovely, she looked lovely at this moment in a new, special way. The fancy pants covered her very tidily. Not a hint of bareness could be seen on her ass, her hips, or of course her more intimate areas. She was totally contained – but oh, how vividly. Her feminine shape and her female sensuality were emphasized rather than obscured by these snug-fitting, ruffle-embellished underpants. There was the subtle roundness of her bottom – tightly clothed. There was the place where her thighs ended, in a geography that could only be a woman's – a geography covered enticingly in nylon vegetation. With giddy ruffles decorating her topography, she looked like a carnival, like a feast. I relished the prospect of fondling every bit of lace, of letting her feel my fingers through the soft interface of the alluring garment.

She paraded in front of the bed, sweetly and shyly, with only a hint of exhibitionistic flair. She spun and shimmied, letting me enjoy the aerodynamic sizzle of the fluttering ruffles, which reminded me of the thin metal jingles on a tambourine. How I wanted to play Megan's percussion!

As if she had read my mind, Megan began to dance gracefully toward the bed in double-time, her hands on her knees and her sassy rear pointed my way. I gave her the gentle slap she was inviting – right on the ruffles – and she rewarded me with a sensuous "Ooh!" Then she turned around and sat in my lap.

The feeling of her lace and nylon on my upper thighs was ticklishly delicious, and I felt every one of my leg hairs tingling. Meanwhile, the pressure of Megan's firm ass cheeks against the bulge in my briefs was pushing me into high gear. With a compulsive enthusiasm, I began to caress her all over her sissy pants, stroking and petting and teasing her from hips to bottom to mound, passionately stimulating her panty-clad flesh.

As she gave in to sensation, Megan quivered, melted, and leaned into me. At this angle, her delicate breasts pressed against my bare chest, and I knew it was time to honour them. I shaped and fondled them with reverence, pinching the nipples lightly in passing.

By now, I was too big for my breeches, and Megan slid my briefs down and away. Below the waist, I saw that she was gyrating.

"So," I said between kisses to her neck. "What's going on in Aunt Clarissa's panties these days?"

"Mmm … something nice," Megan replied.

I reached a hand between her thighs, to stroke the nylon right where it most counted. I felt her softness, her delicacy. The contact made me sigh. "You always feel so very *female* when I touch you there," I commented.

"What can I say," she answered breathlessly. "It's a girl thing."

Her wit sent my arousal soaring even further. Delirious, I stroked her again, and this time she moaned and clutched my shoulders.

"Wow, I'm wet," she whispered a moment later. "I'm sliding all over these now."

She stood up and hooked her fingers into the waist of Aunt Clarissa's panties. Artistically she removed them, by means of a series of sinuous wiggles. Then she turned to me, nude and poised, the glint of her eyes matching the glistening of her pussy. "I think we both agree that those are very special panties," she said dramatically. "But the time for panties has passed, my friend."

As I fell backwards onto the mattress and grabbed Megan's cheerful, bare bottom, I wondered what else Aunt Clarrie might have had in her collection. And as Megan descended onto my precious arousal with the cavity of her moist luxury – and as she began to hump me toward her first frantic climax – my mind reeled with visions of soft black lace on quivering womanly flesh. And as I released into her and her feminine muscles spasmed with joy, I thought I heard the jingling of a hundred pretty tambourines echoing through the house.

It was one of life's marvellous little coincidences that Clarissa's letter arrived the very next day:

Dearest Megan,

Well, it's been another week of gorgeous California

178

weather. I hope you're keeping warm where you are!

There's a little thing I keep meaning to mention, but I always seem to run out of time (or stationery!) before I get to it. So on this occasion, I vowed that I would begin with it ...

Now that your mother's house is all yours, you might keep your eyes open for something that once belonged to me. An article of underwear, if you can believe it! Specifically, my dear niece, I refer to a pair of black rhumba panties. I'm sure you have no idea what those are, and even if you did you would probably just laugh at them. But I hope you'll at least accept the fact that they are NOT a figment of your aunt's imagination. In fact, though I shudder to think that the undies that I wore (it seems) just yesterday are now classified as "vintage," I understand that this style has become quite "collectible", as they say.

If you happen to come across them, you should know that I left them there – accidentally at first, but then intentionally – many years ago. I'm not sure I should really be telling you this whole story ... but you're my favourite person to tell stories to, and it wouldn't seem fair to hold out on you, darling. You see, these panties went missing when I was a young woman, around the time I paid a visit to your parents – who were then newlyweds. I soon forgot all about my rhumba panties ... until another visit some ten years later, during which your mother confessed over afternoon coffee that she'd found them within a week of my losing them, but that she'd been so fascinated by them she had found herself unable to send them on to me! Don't you dare tell her I told you this, but she even admitted that she had tried them on. I was surprised but rather delighted (this was a side of Suburban Big Sister I'd never seen before), and I told her she could keep them, with my blessing.

I have acquired many articles of sexy underwear in my time (most recently last weekend, when my beau Gary and I went shopping together!), and the rhumba panties are not regretted. For all I know, your mother eventually discarded them. In any event, I doubt she made a point of hauling them off to Florida with her, because at this point they (ahem) probably wouldn't fit her so well. But in case they ever turn up in your house, I just wanted you to know that you can get some nice cash for them from a vintage-clothing dealer – consider it extra birthday money from me! Actually, it would please me very much if you liked the panties enough to keep them – YOU they would fit, my dear – but this is merely the wishful thinking of an ageing auntie. All I can say is, I personally had some very good times in those panties. (So don't knock 'em if you haven't tried 'em, kiddo.)

Gary and I are going up to Vancouver next week ...

Sweets
by Elizabeth Cage

"I haven't seen that thong before."

"Yes, you have. At least twice."

"Oh."

And so began our lovemaking. On a sore note, I have to say. I had bought a red lacy thong because he said red underwear turned him on. Perhaps he was colour blind. Can you be colour blind about red? Sometimes, I wondered how much Carl really noticed me; he never *devoured* me sexually, never made me feel that he was *hungry* for me. Sometimes I just wished he would rip all my clothes off.

Don't get me wrong. I'm not being critical. Well, I suppose I am. But I like to try new things, experiment. *Suck it and see* is my favourite catchphrase. The problem we had was the way we each thought about sex. I wanted a gourmet meal whereas Carl was content with a plate of egg and chips.

Thinking back, I can recall at least a couple of occasions when I experienced a sensual pleasure that didn't include actual sex. Like the heavenly banana and chocolate cake I consumed at the a gorgeous upmarket café in Hampstead, and the time that my beloved black cat, Vellore, decided to clean between my toes with her tongue. The toes are a sensitive erogenous zone, and she licked slowly and deliberately between each one with her peach-skin tongue.

Now *that* was sensual.

Of course, I couldn't exactly tell Carl that my cat turned me on more than he did. Particularly when he had been so good to me, lending me money when I lost my job, and putting down the rent deposit on the new apartment we had just moved in to. I managed to get a temporary job at a local beauty salon, thanks to a contact of Carl's, and things seemed to be looking up again when Vellore, who still hankered after my old garden flat, went missing.

"I've been back to my old place, alerted the new tenants, but there's been no sign of her," I told Carl anxiously a week after her disappearance. I was horrified at his response.

"I expect she got run over," Carl replied, then more tenderly, "Don't cry, Kandi. You can always get another cat, you know."

"I could never replace Vellore," I howled.

"No. You're right," he said quickly. "Best not to try." Then he tried to comfort me by cradling my head in his lap, and slowly I began to relax as his fingertips stroked my face and gently pushed back my hair. I was grateful to have him with me in my misery.

As the weeks passed, and Vellore did not return, I told myself that I was lucky to have someone who cared enough to occasionally buy me roses and chocolate truffles and – to my surprise – a pair of crotchless knickers. He was trying hard; you had to give him that. I knew Carl wasn't my soulmate and our relationship lacked passion, but I decided that this was as good as it would get.

Recently, Carl had been staying extra late at the office, and when he finally got home he was usually so tired that any kind of sex was out of the question, let alone anything vaguely kinky. He had been working so hard since his promotion that I decided to do something special for him. Unfortunately, it was my motivation to do good that led to my fateful encounter with Wesley.

I had planned a surprise candle-lit dinner in the flat. Being a hopeless cook, I bought the food from M & S, chose suitable background music from my CD collection and decided to put on some sexy underwear. He was getting the works. However, I wanted to buy something really erotic that he wouldn't forget, so I called in to our local Pillow Talk store to choose an appropriate outfit. They had everything – pretty sensual lingerie, leopard print sheath dresses, latex catsuits, leather thigh boots with stiletto heels, black lace-top stockings, shimmering G-strings, edible condoms … I felt like a kid who had just been given an enormous jar of her favourite sweets.

"Can I help you?"

The guy behind the counter gave a friendly smile. He was tall and good looking, with dark eyes and liquorice black hair. He wore skinny jeans and a black T-shirt which showed off his muscular, tattooed forearms.

"Well, I…"

"Looking for anything in particular?"

"Something sexy," I ventured like a burbling idiot.

"You've come to the right place then," he replied, without a trace of sarcasm. "If you don't mind me making a few suggestions, the black rubber mini-skirt is one of our best sellers," and he scooped one off the rack and handed it to me. "I think you'll find that will fit."

I clutched it to my breasts, my eyes scanning the array of whips and bondage gear displayed on the wall to my right. "Here, try this," he continued, passing me a red silky package, "and these," adding a pair of six-inch spike heels with a complicated arrangement of leather straps. "The changing room is just through here," and he pulled back a black rubber curtain that led into a small cubicle with a gothic-style mirror.

"Need any help to get undressed?" he asked, confidence oozing. "Well, just shout if you need me. I won't be far."

And he hovered outside the cubicle, watching me, until I pulled the curtain shut.

I realised I was trembling. He was a real charmer, an outrageous flirt, but at this moment I didn't mind at all. Quite the opposite, in fact. Somehow, he had managed to choose the right sizes, just by looking at me. And the *way* he looked at me. Lustful without being sleazy. I sighed. Carl never looked at me like that. I wriggled into the skirt, wrestled with the strappy red top and tottered before the mirror in the stiletto bondage shoes.

"Does everything fit?" he called and I knew he was still standing just behind the curtain.

"Yes, but I'm not too sure about…"

"Don't be shy." He pulled back the curtain. "Wow!"

I couldn't move. I had never felt so self-conscious in all my life.

"You look fabulous," he whispered, standing so near that I could feel his breath on the back of my neck.

"You would say that," I muttered. "You're the salesman."

But when I glanced at my reflection I could see that he was right. I did look stunning. A sex goddess. I was gobsmacked.

"Tell me your name," he insisted gently, moving closer.

"K-Kandi."

"Well, K-Kandi, I'm Wesley – let me adjust the straps on this for a perfect fit," and his fingers skilfully tightened the silk ribbons, brushing lightly on my breasts before standing back to admire his work.

"And now the shoes."

I stood motionless, my heart thumping wildly as he crouched down on the floor and pulled in the straps on the fetishy shoes, pausing to let his lips touch my ankles, then kissing my legs and my knees, travelling up to my trembling thighs and belly until I was shaking uncontrollably. He looked up at me and smiled.

"Shall we go for a ride, my sweet?"

At this point I was no longer K-Kandi but had been taken over by Kaaaandi, my newly discovered alter ego. We left in my car and parked on a dirt-track off Bluebell Woods. Wesley smiled. "You look beautiful, Kandi," he murmured, running his fingers down my cheek and I realised sadly that Carl hardly ever used my name when we had sex.

"I'd love to see your body," continued Wesley, sliding a silky strap gently down my shoulder. I lifted my arms and he slipped the red camisole top over my head. It was a warm summer evening but I could feel my skin prickling with goosebumps. And anticipation.

"Hmmmm." He breathed in my scent and kissed me tenderly on the lips before slowly peeling down the rubber skirt. I was naked. In every sense.

"Perfect," he said approvingly, admiring my smooth, shaved pussy. "Your skin," he murmured, devouring me with his mouth. "You taste sweet, like candy." I leaned back, my naked flesh sliding on the leather seat, every sensation heightened, allowing myself to luxuriate in his penetrating kisses. His hand was moving between my thighs, quickly discovering how wet I was already.

He grinned. "You're streaming, Kandi? Did you know that?"

I nodded and groaned as his head moved down and his tongue began to stroke my clitoris in slow rhythmic movements, sending electric currents pulsing through my body while his hands cupped my breasts, his thumbs playing with my nipples. Just when I thought I could bear it no longer he stopped abruptly, leaving me begging for more, while he placed my fingers over his throbbing erection. I ached to feel him inside me, filling and stretching me.

"Fuck me," I whispered. He smiled as I pulled him urgently towards me and soon he was pumping vigorously.

185

I clutched his back, moaning and sobbing.

"Fuck me, fuck me harder," I demanded greedily, my muscles tightening around him.

I was near to coming when he suddenly produced a pair of handcuffs and I readily allowed him to fasten them on to my wrists, the unforgiving metal clicking shut, before he pinned my hands above my head, still thrusting energetically. I loved the delicious feeling of being captive, of giving myself to Wesley. I had often fantasised about such things and it seemed all my erotic dreams were coming true at once – sex with a stranger, in a car, in a deserted spot, handcuffed.

Wesley smiled as I writhed and groaned with pleasure, and now that I was at his mercy, he took charge, slowing down his thrusts, moving in and out of me with careful and deliberate precision, so that I could feel every movement, savouring the gentle and exquisite friction.

"Please," I groaned, desperate to come.

"Soon," he whispered "but not yet."

And he covered my mouth with his, his tongue plunging deeply in contrast to the gentle pulsing of his ramrod cock.

I wanted him to eat me alive, I wanted our bodies to be tied together so we could be coupled like this for ever. Suddenly, he pulled out, leaving me gasping with frustration and surprise. But before I could protest, he tilted my chin upwards and held his glistening cock an inch from my mouth.

"Taste me. Taste yourself on me," he said and I began to suck and gorge greedily while his right hand curled between my thighs, lightly brushing my aching clit, then pushing deeper, finger fucking me until I thought I could hold back no longer.

"Not yet," he whispered once more, withdrawing his cock from my gaping red mouth.

I was trembling now, losing control, and he gripped my ankles and carefully prised my legs even further apart before he bent forward and slid his tongue between my moist lips. As he traced circles around my clit, my back arched as I was overwhelmed by rapidly spiralling sensations and I heard myself cry out as a mind-blowing orgasm wracked my body.

Wesley lifted his head and I noticed that his mouth was smeared with my juices.

"Sweet. Candy sweet," he said.

Momentarily exhausted, I stretched out across the car seat, my wrists still cuffed, while Wesley gently stroked my back and nibbled my neck and it wasn't long before I was ready for more. Besides, this time I wanted to feel Wesley's come explode inside me.

"Round two?" he grinned.

This time he slid into me from behind. I could feel his balls slapping against my buttocks as he thrust excitedly, his breath hot against my neck, and I imagined we were voracious, primitive animals, devouring and being devoured.

"Harder. Fuck me harder," I urged and he pumped more vigorously, grunting and panting while I moaned with pleasure. I had decided I had discovered fuck heaven when Wesley announced irritably, "I think someone's watching us."

"I don't care," I mumbled incoherently, only seconds away from another climax.

"Well, I do," he declared in a macho tone. "I don't want some perv spying on us. I'll go and sort him out."

And before I could stop him, he unceremoniously pulled out, and hastily dressed, despite my protests.

"Back in a minute," he whispered, kissing me on the forehead. "Don't go away."

Then he opened the car door, promptly tripped on a tree root and fell flat on his face. Everything went quiet.

"Wesley?" I peered out furtively. He was lying face down, perfectly still. "Wesley?"

I searched around for my abandoned clothes and retrieved the rubber skirt, which I tried to hitch up to cover my exposed breasts, not easy when you're handcuffed. Then I crawled out of the car and shook Wesley in a desperate attempt to wake him up.

"Wesley, get up, stop messing about," I pleaded, turning him over, but he appeared to be out cold. So, here I was, in the middle of nowhere, semi-naked and alone. Handcuffed. Not really the kind of excitement I had craved. Everything was going horribly wrong. I imagined the newspaper headlines, my workmates reading about my erotic adventures, or worse, my mum! Then a chilling thought crossed my mind. Wesley had gone after a voyeur. Which meant whoever was watching could still be out there right now, waiting, observing my predicament. Perhaps enjoying it. I peered furtively into the gathering darkness and shuddered. Seeing poor Wesley lying there, I made a pathetic but unsuccessful attempt to lift him, but the sound of a twig snapping sent me scurrying back to the car in panic. What a nightmare! I hit the central locking, desperately needing to feel safe. As I shivered, wallowing in self-pity, I thought of Carl, and was overcome with guilt. Surely he would be worrying about me? How long would he wait before contacting the police? I was just considering if it would be possible to drive while handcuffed when I noticed headlights in the distance. When I recognised the markings of a police car I didn't know whether to laugh with relief or die of embarrassment.

A middle-aged uniformed officer flashed his torch and walked cautiously over, nearly tripping over the prostrate Wesley. "I can't wake him. I think he's concussed," I wailed, my voice breaking.

And then the words just came tumbling out. "I was lost. I turned off the road to look at a map and then a big scary guy came from nowhere, handcuffed me and overpowered me. I was terrified. I didn't know what he was going to do."

"*This* man?" asked the policeman, gesturing towards the motionless Wesley.

I shook my head. "No. He tried to help me, pulled off my attacker who then hit him over the head."

"And where is this attacker now?"

"He ran off when he saw your headlights."

I don't know where the story came from. I had never thought of myself as having much of an imagination before but it was quite a convincing scenario, nonetheless. Even so, the officer looked sceptical. "Sounds like you had a lucky escape, Miss."

"Yes," I replied sheepishly.

I still felt pretty dazed when the policeman dropped me back at the flat. I was worried about Wesley and feeling guilty about Carl, who I imagined would be waiting anxiously, so I was rather surprised to find the flat in darkness. God, he was working late again! Then I found the note on the table.

Dear Kandi, I don't know how to tell you this but...

The funny thing was, the same night that Carl left me for his Marketing Assistant, my cat Vellore came back.

Thankfully, Wesley's concussion wasn't serious. I visited him in hospital and it turned out he couldn't remember a thing about what had happened. He was back at work within the week.

I'm going back to the shop today, to buy a set of handcuffs. Perhaps I can do something to jog his memory … after all, we never finished Round Two.

Sonja's Sauna
by Roger Frank Selby

The mobile vibrated on the wooden floor. Erik stirred and glanced over the edge of his bed. The face was lit. A text from… Sonja:

> *Hi Erik, Otto*
> *away4week.*
> *U r invited 2 more*
> *sauna fun!*
> *Bring friend. XS*

Two weeks had passed since the wonderful antics in her sauna where it became clear that she and husband Otto had a very open arrangement. Otto hadn't been away then – the big German had spanked his Swedish wife right there in the sauna, after she'd confessed to "teasing Erik" during their training flight together. And then the fun had really started.

His new girlfriend Tanya was rightly suspicious but Erik had made it clear that Sonja was a friend he simply wouldn't give up – for the moment. He hoped someday to take Tanya to Sonja's sauna – but knew that Otto's presence would inhibit her. (Even his presence inhibited her!)

So this was crunch time. He sent a brief reply but kept Tanya in the dark until they were airborne next day.

'Aren't we somewhere near that Shepherd's Farm place, Erik?'

Although she'd only heard that airfield mentioned once before on the radio, she'd remembered it and its link to his female flying instructor. Smart girl.

'Ja, I mean yeah; it's the airstrip that belongs to Sonja's husband – our destination on today's mystery tour!'

'Oh.'

She didn't sound too pleased.

'Sonja has invited us for a sauna. You said you didn't mind saunas?'

'I don't, but I didn't bring my swimsuit.'

'We aren't going swimming!'

'But I don't have anything to wear – you should have warned me!'

'And spoiled a nice surprise? No way!'

At last she smiled. He set up his final approach over the marching pylons and into the short strip. As the little Robin rumbled onto the grass, Erik saw Sonja waving from the apron in front of the big open barn that served as a hangar. The barn was empty. He'd heard at the flying club that Otto had taken his huge Turbo-Porter 'meat bombing' in German skies – dropping skydivers from high altitude.

He applied a short burst to set the machine trundling towards the bikini-clad woman, who now had her hands on her hips. Apart from the skimpy yellow bikini, she was wearing an uncharacteristic frown. Uh-ho, what was the problem? Of course! She had assumed he would bring a *male* friend. Oops.

He gave a brief smile and waved through the canopy as he shut down and finished his checks.

'She doesn't seem very pleased to see me,' announced Tanya.

'No, it's not you – probably the way I did my approach and landing. She is still my instructor, even though I have my licence now.' If only that *were* the problem, but it might serve as a distraction until Sonja got used to Tanya being his 'friend'.

He finally opened the bubble canopy to the glorious summer's day. 'Hi Sonja – yeah, sorry about that ragged approach and landing – but it was my first one handling the controls into "Shepherd's."' He gave her the slightest of winks.

Sonja was a smart woman too, and immediately fell into the ploy. 'Ja Erik, we maybe talk later about it over beer, but now you must introduce me to your friend.' She was almost smiling, shielding her eyes from the sun, as if that had been why she'd been frowning. Clever; and what a wonderful shape that swimsuit barely concealed. He well remembered how that shape had looked (and felt) unconcealed.

'Sonja, this is my friend Tanya. Tanya, this is my flying instructor, Sonja, the lady who dragged me through my PPL course.'

'Hi Sonja – I've seen you around at the club.'

'Hi Tanya. Ja, I have seen you there with Erik. Well, don't just sit there on ceremony, jump out both of you and come to my sauna!'

Well, thought Tanya, maybe it *was* the sun in her eyes, or Erik's flying, because now Sonja was being the perfect, smiling hostess, as they entered the small building by the farmhouse.

'And now, all men will wait outside the changing room while us girls get changed, right Tanya?'

'Right!'

Erik grinned ruefully as Sonja closed the door on him – rather roughly, Tanya thought.

'Er, I'm afraid I don't have a swimsuit, Sonja,' she appealed to the older woman. 'Erik, bless him, didn't tell me where we were going – It was a "mystery tour"!'

'But you and Erik, you are...' Sonja appeared to stop

192

herself saying something indiscreet as she took off her bikini top. 'No problem, I lend you something, you are close to my size, I think.'

Well, close enough, thought Tanya, although Sonja was perhaps more well-developed than her in the jiggling bust now exposed to her.

Tanya turned modestly away as she shed her own clothes and donned the costume Sonja handed her. When safely installed, she turned to face the Swede's appraisal.

'There, you fit my swimsuit very well.'

Tanya glanced down at her own body. Erik had never seen her in swimwear before. She hoped he would be pleased with her, especially with Sonja more or less topless, with maybe just the ends of that towel covering her conical nipples.

They walked through, into the wooden heat of the sauna itself.

'OK, Erik,' Sonja called out, 'Girls are going into sauna; you can come in and change now.'

They sprawled on the benches, and Erik joined them a minute or two later, looking quite beautiful with just a towel wrapped around his waist. Tanya watched his eyes as he glanced first at Sonja's half-covered bosom, and then at her. He seemed slightly disappointed to see both women somewhat covered up, but he did a kind of double-take on her as he sat down nearby.

'Wow, Tanya, did Sonja lend you that?'

'Do you like it, then?' She lay back a little more, her breasts rising.

'I love the way you look in it – first time I've seen you in a swimsuit.'

'Thanks, Erik.'

'Well, swimsuits are not really for saunas,' added Sonja, 'they are for swimming. And in sauna, you wear only until everybody is comfortable and relaxed in the heat. When so, and all are friends, it is better with no swimsuits, I think.'

We'll see about that, thought Tanya.

'Who would like steam?' asked Sonja jumping up. Immediately her towel ceased any covering function – bobbing breasts nudged the towel curtain aside and displayed themselves to the guests.

'Yes, please.'

'Er, just a minute, Tanya,' interrupted Erik, dragging his eyes from Sonja's jiggling bosom, 'It will feel ten times hotter with steam – wet heat is the killer in saunas; we want to keep it dry for a while at least.'

And maybe it would kill any sexual high jinks too, she thought. 'Better not then; thanks anyway, Sonja.'

'OK. Erik is maybe right if this your first time.'

Sonja returned to the bench easing her bikini briefs off her hips, and covering her lap with a towel as she sat. She pushed the briefs down her legs and bent to retrieve them, breasts swinging spectacularly.

Sitting there in the heat, Tanya felt overdressed. Oh well, Erik had seen her semi-naked in previous skirmishes, and she had been bare-breasted in the changing room with Sonja – time to show her tits a little, perhaps… but no. She had an urge to do so but she would like Erik to do the revealing – maybe touch her in the process…

She couldn't believe how bold she was feeling. Why?

It must be Sonja. Somehow she trusted this sensuous woman. She felt secure while she was there. A sort of safety in numbers – not that she distrusted Erik.

She looked up at him and smiled. He grinned back.

'Do you think I'm overdressed?' she asked him.

'Maybe – but no pressure, Tanya. Like Sonja says, when you're relaxed…'

'But I am relaxed, Erik. I'm so relaxed I don't want to move a muscle – and how can I undress without moving?' In the brief silence that followed, she watched his towel rising in his lap.

His eyes were fixed on her. 'I could undress you.'

She glanced at Sonja and saw that she had her full attention too. Sonja laughed. 'I wish I had kept some clothes on – then he could have undressed me too.'

'Come on then, Erik, what's stopping you?'

'Nothing much, Tanya.' He stood up, struggling to cover his growing erection with the towel. It was a losing battle.

'I would say that is much better than nothing much,' commented Sonja, drily. Still sitting, she reached forward, caught the edge of the towel and snatched it from him.

Tanya found herself going along with Sonja's prank, giggling at the sudden revelation. Erik shrugged and approached Tanya naked, his male member pointing up at her face, swinging, from side to side with each step.

The sight frightened her a little but Sonja was there and Erik was more embarrassed than the enthralled women – Sonja looked hypnotized by the sight.

Tanya thrust out her covered breasts, inviting them to be touched by the naked man. Erik seemed to hesitate, maybe because Sonja was watching.

'You must feel her, Erik.'

He reached out and gently held her left breast in both his hands. Tanya revelled in the all-enveloping touch, the gentleness of it.

'Now the other one,' prompted Sonja.

He grasped her covered right breast in a similar fashion, but Tanya felt his increased urgency as he squeezed it a little harder.

'And now you must undo her.'

Erik leaned over her to reach the fastening. She leaned forward so he could reach behind her as she sat, and her mouth was very close to the swaying tip. Sonja's view was blocked by Erik, so she couldn't see Tanya's full lips opening and going down over the swollen head. She took him in a little way into her mouth. She heard him gasp. She ran her tongue over the tip and tasted him.

At that same moment, she felt the back strap of the

195

bikini top come undone and her breasts surge forward.

Maybe Sonja couldn't see, but she must have heard Erik gasp, then sigh as he gathered Tanya's released breasts in his hands…

But here was Sonja! She stood naked beside the pair of them. She could see everything.

'Ah ha! You have your man where you want him, Tanya!'

Tanya couldn't speak with her mouth full; she just made an 'Mmmm' sound. Erik was glad she made no attempt to take her mouth away from its important work on him.

This was a first! Sonja's presence seemed to be stimulating Tanya. He wondered how she would deal with him touching Sonja, if it came to that…

'Can I touch him too, Tanya?'

'Mmmm.'

Sonja touched him. She fondled his bottom from the side with one hand and then leaned over, reaching down with the other. He felt the fingertips touch him gently, lifting the loose contents of his sac.

With Sonja's large breasts pressed against his side, Erik had a spare hand and handled both women, comparing them, Tanya being only a little smaller and delightfully pointier.

After a few minutes of being fondled and sucking, Tanya came up for air. Still holding him she looked up at him with heavy-lidded eyes. Then she glanced across at Sonja.

Erik followed her gaze. Sonja was looking wistfully at his fully extended cock in the other woman's grasp. He felt a twinge as his flesh responded to squeezing fingers.

'I have a nice game for us girls – we will blindfold the man – and he will guess which girl!'

Tanya did not look so sure. She was being very territorial with Erik's territory.

'I have even better idea, then – screen, not blindfold!' She pointed to the end of the sauna. Erik noticed a padded bench, from an old gym maybe, about knee-height. Beside and above it there was something that looked like a shower curtain rail, with a black shower curtain furled to one side. Sonja bounced over to it and pulled out the dark screen along the edge of the bench.

There was a slit in the screen at groin height...

With an erotic shock to his loins, Erik got the idea.

The idea was made even plainer when Sonja climbed onto the bench on her hands and knees, the tips of her breast swinging just above the padded surface, her bottom backing up to the slot in the screen.

'You get up on this bench with me, Tanya?'

'No... sorry, Sonja...' Clearly she was not ready for this advanced stage yet – she still had her bikini bottoms on. He also noticed she had released her grip on him.

Sonja seemed stricken but she remained exactly where she was, with her bare bottom stuck out invitingly. 'I am sorry, Tanya; I'm so naughty... I wish Otto were here, he would spank me for this... in front of both of you!' An idea seemed to strike her. She looked pleadingly at the younger woman. 'Would you let Erik spank me instead?'

'Let Erik spank you?'

'Yes. I need this... now.'

'Well... OK.' Tanya looked intrigued – and perhaps relieved to be a mere spectator for a while.

Without wishing to appear too enthusiastic in front of Tanya, Erik stepped up to the bench and drew the screen aside to perform his duty. His cock showed his true enthusiasm, swinging stiffly about the upward vertical as he moved into position. He felt a desperate need to penetrate Sonja, with her broad bottom presented at convenient cock-height – only inches away from his inches.

He stood slightly to one side as Tanya moved closer to watch. 'Ready?'

'Yes, spank me as hard as you saw Otto spank me.'

'But that was the one thing Otto would not let me...'

'Otto is not here.'

It's all coming out now, thought Tanya, with a bounding of her heart. She still didn't know exactly what had happened between Erik and Sonja on previous occasions but now she knew for sure that he had witnessed a wifely spanking, at the very least. What else had happened?

With a thrill she watched Erik's hands spread and hold the woman's prominent buttocks, as if gauging their softness for the impending punishment. Then he drew his right hand back.

Smack!

'Ow!'

Smack!

'Ooooh!'

Tanya's heart leapt in her chest as she watched the naked spanking. She wanted to hold Erik's upstanding phallus as it swayed with each smack of his hand, but she couldn't get in close without getting in his way.

She felt herself dripping wet under the constricting bikini briefs and it wasn't just the sweat of the sauna. She eased them down her buttocks and thighs, and saw Erik glance at her pale, freshly bared bottom as she stepped out.

'Want to be spanked too?' He didn't smile.

She was so breathless, she couldn't answer. She nodded.

'Get up here beside Sonja.'

She did so, her behind offered up to the right of Sonja's. There was a pause in Sonja's spanking, and she felt Erik's strong hands on her naked body, gripping and squeezing the broad, soft flesh of her bottom… then:

Smack!

She yelped. A different cry to Sonja's but she knew that she'd been smacked just as hard, and no harder. And then she was lost in a sea of joy as the man spanked the two women equally, spreading his smacks along the four buttocks in turn.

She was amazed. She had no idea that spanking was her 'thing,' until now.

And then, when her bottom felt a warm glow, the spanking stopped. She felt fingers probing her labia. She heard Sonja moan and guessed the same was happening to her.

She held still.

Then the fingers became an unmistakable tongue, lapping and probing her where she wanted to be lapped and probed. But her need was great.

'Fuck me now, Erik.'

At last she was ready for him. He kept his left fingers deep in Sonja and gently engaged his cockhead against Tanya's moist opening. A slight leakage from the tip was lubricant as he pushed into her for the very first time. He smoothly slid all the way up inside the warmth of her.

'Oooooooh. Fuck me, fuck me...' She ground her buttocks around and eased back and forth, using his full length.

He obliged, riding one woman while his fingers probed the other. His free hand gave Tanya's right buttock the occasional hard slap or reached under to catch and squeeze her bouncing breasts. She cried out with each smack and every hard squeeze seemed to energise her more.

After only a few minutes, Tanya came in a series of howling climaxes. He felt her inner muscles squeezing down on him, knowing she would finish way before he was ready for her.

As Tanya slowed her action and relaxed, Sonja asked, quite gently, 'Can Erik fuck me now, Tanya?'

'Ah... yes, OK.'

Never before in his life had Erik transferred from one woman to another like this. Even as he did so, he realised that he had not actually been consulted in the proceedings but treated by these women as a mere fucking machine. He withdrew fully erect, stepped to the left and slid deep, up into Sonja, hardly missing a beat.

'Ooooohh!' Sonja at once became as active as he remembered from last time – perhaps even more so, now that her husband's member was not there to locate her head in one position.

What was this? Tanya was now by Sonja's side and offering him her bountiful breasts as he fucked Sonja. He handled and sucked her pink standing nipples, a sweet accompaniment to the intimacy with the woman beneath.

Sonja was now very close to coming by the feel and the sound of it. As she had done before, she tended to hold her breath and then release it in a shudder as she came. After a few more shudders she was spent and her mobile abdomen slowly ceased its tossing, like a calming sea.

Sonja gave a deep sigh as she un-impaled herself from the man, turned and gazed at his firmness. 'And now the girls need to make the man come. He has satisfied two women and needs his release.'

That sounds like a good idea, thought Erik.

'Why don't you suck your man, Tanya?'

'I will. But not when he …'

'Ah. No problem. I will take over.'

'No. I want to see it …'

'Then I will take over with my hands …'

'Now, just a bloody minute!' Erik had had enough of this. 'I get the idea, and it's very kind of you ladies to try and satisfy me. I will try and do what Tanya wants but first, I want the two of you back where you were so I can move between you … OK?'

'OK.'

'Ja.'

'Right!'

His erection had been fading a trifle but was back to iron condition the moment the two ladies' bare rear-ends presented themselves to it.

Over the next few minutes he indulged himself, moving

in and out of the pussies until he was almost ready to explode. He noticed that Sonja had a small bottle of baby oil in her hand.

'OK!' he withdrew from Tanya and lay back flat on the padded bench as the women gathered around. He felt Tanya's lips and mouth descend on him lovingly for a while, then it was time for the oil.

Sonja's oily hands stroked up and down his vertical shaft with a perfect motion and he knew he was close. Her motion became faster and her tits seemed to bounce around on either side of her work.

'Ahhhh!'

The first jet exploded out of him and slapped against the sauna ceiling.

'Oh!' cried out Tanya, unaware that such things were possible.

'Ahhhhhh!'

The second and third slapped into Sonja's hair and breasts.

'Oooohh!

Part of the fourth spurt caught Tanya's cheek as her lips descended upon him. The rest she took in, while her head bobbed up and down, and Sonja looked on benignly.

The three of them were relaxing in the afterglow when he caught a familiar sound. It was the faint but blaring sound of a turboprop aircraft ... getting louder as it taxied up to the barn.

'Oh God! Otto has come back early!' cried Sonja.

'But he doesn't mind friends in the sauna, does he?' asked Erik.

'He doesn't mind a lot of things – you know this, Erik – but he does not like this ...' (She turned and showed her red smacked-bottom to them both) '... to be done by anyone but Otto!'

'Oh shit,' groaned Erik.

'Quick – rub the oil onto my bottom! It will reduce the marks a little.'

She offered up her behind and they both smoothed in the lotion while she knelt. In a minute or so the hand marks were certainly less distinct than before.

The turbine whine changed abruptly, running down the scale, dying as the fuel was cut. Otto could be looking in any minute now …

'Sit back on the bare wooden bench now, Sonja,' suggested Erik. 'The boards will make stripes that will hide any remaining marks on your bottom.'

They heard the outer door open, and then the hiss of the shower in the changing room. They were sweating innocently on the benches, towels partly covering their nudity, when the sauna door finally opened.

Tanya's eyes opened wide as the blond giant entered, clad in just a tiny towel. She instinctively drew her towel up to cover her bosom.

'Otto, my darling! You are back home early!'

Sonja leapt up into her husband's arms. Towels fell away as they kissed and Otto seemed pleased to see her, Tanya thought, approvingly.

But Sonja's behind, although striped by the bench, still had a pink, just-spanked look about it.

'Ja, the weather in Bavaria is bad for few days. I come home to see my wife … Zo!' he boomed, 'Who are the friends here? Ah – I see Erik! No, don't get up Erik, relax … And, ah-ha! A *zehr schön fraulein!*'

'Tanya, this is my lovely big husband, Otto. Darling, this is Tanya, the friend of Erik's.'

'Enchanté, Tanya.' Otto took her extended hand and kissed it, continental style, as her other hand clutched her towel just above nipple level.

Maybe he was trying to be the total European with a classic French compliment, but she sensed that he would have clicked his heels, had he been shod. Unshod and naked he strolled deeper into the sauna. He ran a brawny, fair-haired paw over the padded bench …

Then he spotted the mark on the ceiling.

His face darkened. He turned and faced Sonja. 'Have you anything to tell me, Wife?'

'I have been naughty, my husband.'

Erik completed his after take-off check and set course for Greenfield. Up to now, Tanya had been very quiet beside him. She seemed lost in thought. He really hoped that this exotic beginning of sex between them wasn't also its ending.

'When I get married I hope to have a relationship just like those two.'

He let out a puff of relief and allowed himself a smile. 'Really? Spanking and everything?'

'Ja!' she laughed.

Levelling off at 2500 feet in the evening sky, he relaxed and set cruise power. 'Sonja saved my bacon back there.'

'By telling Otto it was me who spanked her, not you?

'Yup,' he grinned.

'No. I think it was me who saved you by not denying it, then agreeing to let Otto spank me.'

'And you loved it, didn't you?'

'It was bearable.'

He laughed, and thought of the big wink Otto had tipped him as he spanked the bared Tanya. Otto knew very well that Erik had smacked Sonja's forbidden bottom and chosen the appropriate response.

And Tanya – wow! What a secret woman he'd discovered in her. After her sound spanking by Otto, he wondered if there was something she now needed.

'Erik?'

'Yeah?'

'After we land, can we go straight back to your place?'

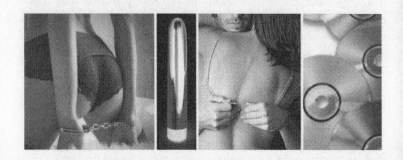